Looks-at-Clouds

Published by Learning Tides Ltd.
www.learningtides.co.uk

Written by Robert Foley
Edited by Jan Rylewicz
Cover Design by Carol Dawson

© 2023 by Learning Tides Ltd.
Clacton-on-Sea, United Kingdom

ISBN 978-1-9993609-6-2

Printed on demand

To the people of the Southern Appalachian Mountains, family and friends who will always hold a special place in my heart. My son, Jacob Samuel Lee Vann, for always encouraging me to write stories, and to Reverend White Bear Barnard, PhD for all his teachings.

'Sacred One, teach us love, compassion, and honor, that we may heal the Earth and each other.'

Melungeon Shapeshifter

Nola Gibson got up early on this beautiful spring morning and cooked breakfast. As always, her dogs Paix and Lassie followed her every step. When she had breakfast prepared, she went to the bedroom door of her grandfather, knocking lightly. "Nonno, are you awake? Breakfast is ready."

In a sleepy voice Nonno said, "Yes, Nola, I'm awake. Just trying to talk these old bones into moving."

Nola replied, "Well, hurkle-durkle, I made gravy, biscuits, fried eggs, and ham. The coffee is ready, so get up and we'll eat, then go vote."

Obert Gibson was now 69 years old and could feel every year in his joints. He lived with his granddaughter Nola on the old family farm, as had several generations before them. Nola worked four days a week as an EMT and went to school to become a nurse.

After breakfast she said, "Nonno, I'll do the dishes. You just shower and get ready. We'll go by and pick up Mr. and Mrs. Jackson and go vote before the polls get crowded."

"What about Mr. Fields? We always take him to vote."

"Nonno, I'll go back and get him…then you, and Mr. and Mrs. Jackson, don't have to smell him. I like Mr. Fields, but he smells like a donniker. Besides, he likes to hang around the polls to see how many half pints of election whiskey he can get for his vote. In the end he'll go vote the way he intended to all along."

Obert huffed, "There are no politics like Kentucky politics, and sure not like Harlan County politics. As for Mr. Fields, his mother was Irish and the Irish love whiskey. Speaking of his mother, her father was the Brennan of their clan. They believe that all forms of matter hold a form of life. It is called *Hylozoism* which is the doctrine held by many early Greek philosophers of all matter containing life."

"Yes, Nonno, I've heard of it, but I'm not sure I agree with it. And with the poor choice of politicians we have these days, I'm not sure I even agree with going to the trouble of voting. After all, we all just have one vote. Those who are running for office don't deserve any."

Obert paused for a moment, choosing his words wisely. "If you walk down to the river and toss a dornick into the water, what will happen?"

"It will splash the water, and ripples will reach out to the shorelines."

"So, your action has an effect on the river?"

Nola thought through the scenario with eyes closed, then said, "Yes, but the ripples fade away and the water is still the same as before."

Obert smiled. "The dornick remains at the bottom of the river, changing its flow ever so slightly. Now, what would happen with lots more dornicks and even larger ones?"

Nola frowned, remaining unconvinced of the value of politics. "I see your point, Nonno. If there are enough, they will soon dam the river and change its flow. Yet how do we know whether this is better?"

"We try to learn as much as we can about issues and candidates, then try to use good judgement and good old fashioned common sense."

"You have convinced me. One vote does matter, after all. Now, let's go vote!"

After going to vote, Nola took Mr. and Mrs. Jackson home. She dropped Nonno off and spent a few more hours taking other folks to vote.

On returning home after a busy morning, Obert and Nola sat on the front porch, sipping lemonade and watching Paix and Lassie play in the yard. She turned to her grandfather, with new, pressing questions. "Nonno, do you think mom and dad are happy in the world of the ancients?"

He raised his bulky, unkempt eyebrows. "I'm sure they are…other than that they really miss you."

Nola asked, "Do you think they could have lived longer in this world, before having to transition to the ancient one?"

"No, granddaughter, they were exposed to too much radiation. Darned cancer was eating their health away."

"Will they live forever in the ancient world?"

Obert knew that there was a discrepancy between the word *forever*, and any experience that awaited beyond the visible world, so he was careful in his response. "Well, I don't know about forever, but they will live for a very long time before moving to the next level. And who knows, maybe that will be forever. When we hiked up into the mountains above Quadrule Falls, I watched them transition to open the portal to the ancient world. I had also transitioned to help them get closer to it, because they were very weak. I witnessed the vortex but kept back from it so as not to pass through the portal myself. If so, I could not have come back to be in this world with you. Just briefly, I saw them on the other side of it, where they were instantly young and healthy, as you remember them."

Nola looked over to her grandfather a little fearfully. "You told me the next time you transition you will have to go into the portal."

"Yes, I will, but I don't plan to transition for a very long time. That's why I have always advised you not to transition as often as I did. It is painful and very dangerous in the world of today. There are too many people with guns in these mountains."

"Nonno, I promise to always be selective when I transition."

Later in the afternoon, she was busy in the house cooking dinner, while Obert rested on the porch with the dogs. The sheriff's car turned in the driveway and pulled to a stop in front of the house. Obert yelled to Nola, "Here come Sheriff Williams and Deputy Doofus."

Law enforcement officer Williams walked up the porch; before he could speak, Obert raised his gravelly voice, stopping him in his step. "There's no need in coming to try and buy my vote. I already voted for you simply because there was no one better on the ticket."

Sheriff Williams hissed, "You know, Obert, you always confirm what people say about you Melungeons being mean and ornery."

The old man grinned.

"I see you've been polishing that badge to try and hold onto it for another four years. Maybe Deputy Doofus will run against you in the next election to improve the ticket."

Nola yelled from inside the house like a distant referee, "You two old farts better play nice. Don't make me stop my cooking to come out there!"

Obert grinned some more, then blew spit from the corner of his mouth onto the porch. "I'm sure Deputy Doofus would like that just fine."

Nola yells, "Nonno!"

Obert grumbles, then resigns to his granddaughter's appeal to reason. "Okay, okay, I'll try to be nice."

"That would be a first," replies Sheriff Williams.

Nola yells once more, this time more nettled. Cooking is her quiet space, which by contrast calls out the silliness of this petty argument. "Now, Sheriff Williams, that goes for you too. You ain't got no special rights in these parts. Do y'all want to stay for dinner, have some coffee or lemonade?"

"Lemonade sounds good," agreed the sheriff.

"Alright, that wasn't so hard. Three lemonades coming up. You can handle another, can't you, Nonno?"

"Yeah, I can, especially if the good sheriff laces it up a bit with his cheap election whiskey."

"My whiskey ain't cheap," he protested.

Everyone laughed.

Nola joined the men on the front porch with the lemonade. "Okay, sheriff, you didn't come for votes or lemonade, so what are you here for?"

"Old Man Sutton over yonder at the foot of Pine Mountain took his two young grandsons on a hike into the mountains, possibly heading up to Blanton Forest. They never returned last night. We have search teams with dogs out looking for them. We've also had an airplane searching for most of the morning. There has been no sign of them. We hope to locate them before dark. If not, all search teams will have to pull back. According to weather reports, there is a huge line of thunderstorms mixed with tornadoes heading this way. The storm will likely hit around 1:00 or 2:00 a.m."

Obert asked, "Did they take a daypack, any food, water, or a first aid kit? Do you know if Old Man Sutton took a weapon or not? That is bear country, and there are more than enough snakes to go round as well as other critters. And I don't have to tell you that they need to be located before the storm hits."

The sheriff replied, "According to the family, they did take a pack with some food, water, and a small first aid kit. Mr. Sutton always carries a S&W .38 special in his back pocket. Not a bear killer, but it would likely run one off. Obert, the reason I am here is that if we cannot locate them within the next few hours, before it gets dark, then I'd like to get you to find them. You know these mountains better than anyone, and you can put that Melungeon blood to work and track at night. I know you like to work alone but I can offer you some help."

Nola, every bit as practical, spoke up, "Did Mr. Sutton take a cell phone with him?"

"No, he doesn't have one and doesn't believe in using 'em."

Nola nodded. "Sheriff, my grandfather is too old to be roaming through the mountains at night, but I can track almost as good as he can."

Obert shook his head slowly. "Now, granddaughter, let the old man speak for himself."

"No, Nonno, I won't. Not this time. If anyone goes, it will be me."

He knew there was no changing her mind, and relented. "Well now, sheriff, there you have it. If you don't locate them before dark, Nola will go search for them."

"Okay, then. But Nola, why don't you let us send some help with you? The Suttons could have traveled a far piece."

"No thanks," she replied, "I'll track as Nonno always has…alone. It's a family trait."

Sheriff Williams sighed. "You damn Melungeons are as stubborn as mules. But we need to get going. Thanks for the lemonade. I'll call in a few hours and let you know one way or the other."

"Bye, sheriff, and good luck with the election."

Obert piped up, "Yeah, don't forget to polish your badge."

The sheriff smiled at his deputy and drove off.

Nola turned to her grandfather, still uncertain about the nature of the ancient world. "Nonno, I know you don't want me to start transitioning so soon, but please tell me more about it…tell me how it works…and what to expect. And why is the portal above Quadrule Falls? How do I find it?"

"Transitioning is a natural thing for us. We relax our body, press our hands together, look to the heavens, and will it. It's as simple as that. The first time is a little scary and painful. It's the same when we transition back. Once you are in the form of the Ancient Ones, you'll see at night as if it was day. You'll be able to smell better than a bear, and sense intensely the direction of what you desire. You'll have no problem finding Old Man Sutton and his grandchildren, but there is no guarantee you'll find them alive. Be prepared for that just in case."

Obert continued, "You already know to avoid letting anyone see you. Everyone with a gun wants to kill a so-called *Big Foot*. I always carry a small bear-skin pack on me in which I place my clothes and items, so when I locate people, I can change back and not frighten them. Having your items arranged this way can also be helpful if you change back with too many people around." He briefly paused, to mark that he was about to say something significant, something his beloved granddaughter had to pay attention to at all costs. "If you should ever get injured to a degree that is life-threatening, you'll sense how to find a portal. There are many around the world, but the nearest one around here is above Quadrule Falls. If anything should happen, go there and be with your parents and ancestors. We are the direct line of the Ancient Ones, and our kind can be found around the world. The reason that people don't find any of our remains is because we go home when it's time."

Obert added, in an almost lecturing tone, "As you know, we are called many different things…Bigfoot…Sasquatch, Yeti,

Shapeshifter, among many other names. It doesn't matter what we are labeled as, we are who we are. We are here to help take care of people, the animals, and the land. Even though people are afraid of us, we are still meant to help when we can. We fit in well in these mountains with the people they called Melungeons. They are a Cherokee, European, and African mix. Or part Cherokee and Portuguese, or Turkish. I'm sure you've heard it said, that you should better watch those Melungeons from across the mountain, they are a Turkish blend, and you know how them Turks like knives."

Obert calmly, and not without a hint of humour, added, "Melungeons are just a mixed race of people much like the rest of the people in this world. You could say Melungeons are a Heinz 57 race of people. Our features help us blend in well with the Melungeons. Quadrule Falls is named for an almost forgotten, peaceful clan of Indians who once lived in Harlan County. They moved west of the Mississippi River in 1838 when all Native Americans were forced to live on its western side. This was better known as the *Trail of Tears*; however, some of their descendants remain here."

Obert looks at Nola in the manner of a teacher pleased with the reception of his wisdom. He takes a deep breath and says, "Nola, I'll get my pack ready for you in case the sheriff does need your help. It will have all the things you need in it, and room for your clothes."

"Nonno, we should have this kind of conversation more often. I learn so much, and I love learning new nuances of ancient wisdom."

"We don't want to rush things. Keep in mind, each time we transition takes a little time from us in this life. So please don't be as reckless with it as I've been in my lifetime."

"I understand. Now let's go in and have dinner. Preparing it has grabbed time from my life too," laughed Nola.

Just after dinner, the sheriff called to let her know that the Suttons had not been located. Nola told the officer that she'd head out right away to where the Suttons were last seen.

As they were leaving, Obert imparted a last piece of advice to her. "If you should find them alive and it's late, find shelter and wait out the storm."

"I know, Nonno. You've taught me very well."

In the car, he asked his granddaughter to be careful and not to turn on her phone until she was ready to return from the mountains.

"I know. I'll be extra careful. I love you, Nonno. I'll be fine. Please try not to worry."

As she entered the mountain, the feeling of excitement was like nothing she'd ever experienced. She waited until she was well into the deep forest. It was now dark, and being an overcast night sky, and moon and stars only briefly peeking through the clouds, the land seemed even darker. When Nola felt that the time was right, she removed all her clothes and placed everything in the bear-skin pack.

She placed her hands together, looked up at the sky and started her transformation. Just as her grandfather had told her, it felt scary and painful, yet was quickly completed. She was surprised to find her senses overly keen, and the physical strength within her was overwhelming.

Nola now moved very quickly towards Blanton Forest. She could see clearly. She knew in an instant that she was the supreme being of the forest. She came upon a junction in the trail and knew the Suttons had passed in this direction. Roughly two hours later, she smelled and heard them.

She sensed the storm getting closer. It would soon arrive. As Nola moved towards the lost persons, she reached a large cliff overhang. A small fire was smouldering beneath it, and she saw children moving about. With a sigh of relief, she noted they at least had shelter and warmth.

She knew it was time to transition back, but she wasn't looking forward to giving up the strength and abilities she now possessed. Still, she had to yield them. She transformed back, got dressed, turned her light on and yelled for the Suttons. The children replied, "Over here, over here."

Nola approached and asked, "Is everyone okay?"

The older boy said, "Yes, but grandpa fell and broke his leg. He has been sick."

Nola put her pack down and removed the first aid kit. She said to the children, "Get some food and water from my pack, and I will look after your grandfather."

Nola addressed Mr. Sutton in a gentle tone, "I'll get you fixed up, and get you and the children home as soon as I can. You picked a good place to shelter, and we do have a storm moving in. We'll have to wait it out. I'll call for help in the morning and get you and the children off this mountain."

Mr. Sutton replied, "I guess I'm getting too old to wander around in these parts. I stepped on a loose rock, fell, and broke my leg…been running a fever also. I was afraid to send the children off the mountain by themselves. I knew this place, so I thought we'd hunker down here and wait until someone came looking for us."

"That was good thinking. This is a good place to shelter. However, search teams have been scouring the wrong area of the forest. I have a phone, but I cannot get a signal here. In the morning, I'll walk up the ridge and call for help."

Nola quickly gathered more wood for the fire and made the children and Mr. Sutton as comfortable as possible. The storm hit and passed over by first light. She went up the ridge and called for help, giving the sheriff their GPS location. By midday, all souls were safely off the mountain.

Obert was there, waiting for her. "I was worried. Did everything go okay?"

"Yes, everything worked out just fine. I didn't want to change back. I liked the feeling of being strong and sure of myself."

"Tell me about it. Yet it is just how things have to be and are meant to be."

"But Nonno, I still don't understand why people are so afraid of us when we only want to help."

"Granddaughter, folks tend to be afraid of someone or something they see as different and can't explain. And honestly, I don't think people will ever change."

"Still, I simply feel invigorated and excited. Will that feeling go away?"

Obert said, "Yes, granddaughter, at least to a large degree. For now, you'll go back to being a Melungeon. You'll become a nurse and will still help people. I believe our purpose in life is to learn and help teach others the true meaning of love and kindness. Remember, our values define who we are, not what we look like. Always look for the good in people, and let your life be filled with wonder."

Mountain Folklore

In the Southern Appalachian Mountains of the United States of America lives a unique breed of people. They have over time mixed with many different cultures and developed into one uniquely their own.

The Cherokee as well as other roaming tribes originally inhabited these mountains. But with European contact, their way of mountain life quickly changed.

The Irish came and brought with them their Gaelic language and customs; as did the British, Scots, Germans, Scots-Irish, Welsh, and many others. All immigrants brought with them their diverse customs and culture. It seems that the Irish and Scots-Irish adapted more quickly to the mountains and hills of Southern Appalachia.

It has been said for generations, that when the English first came to Appalachia, they built fine churches. The Germans built big, beautiful barns, and the first things the Irish built were moonshine stills.

It was a rough life, and mere survival was difficult. These migrants mixed with the Cherokees and other Native American tribes, contributing their cultures as they wanted to make life more bearable, and safer, for their families.

The Removal Bill was passed by the U.S. Congress in 1830, but was fought in the courts until 1838, when many Native Americans were relocated west of the Mississippi River. If the government knew that one had as little as one percent Native American blood, the person was forced to relocate. In defiance of the U.S. Government, many Native Americans fled to the mountains of Southern

Appalachia, where some had mixed families or friends, attempting to deny any degree of Native American heritage. These people started using terms such as *Black Irish*, *Black Dutch*, *Portuguese*, or several other nationalities, to deny their heritage.

At the same time, the United States Government did not care who inhabited the sparsely populated mountainous region of Southern Appalachia. Nothing there seemed of value.

Music has always been, and always will be, a huge part of mountain life. The fiddle, harmonica, guitar, bagpipes, drums, banjo, and dulcimer, along with lots of singing, formed a big part of the culture. Front porch bands, as they became known, were very common. Fireside storytelling was also a favorite pastime. By the mid-1800s to the early 1900s, many different cultures had blended into one uniquely of its own.

It is common to see local front-and back porch ceilings painted light blue to keep evil spirits from entering a house. Chimes on the porch are another means to ward off evil spirits. It is common to see a crucifix, an image of Jesus Christ, and a Native American medicine wheel or dream catcher, hanging in the same room. Most often, a family Bible is placed in the living room of homes. This is where births and deaths are recorded for future generations. It is also where one can obtain information about ancestors.

Funeral traditions are changing somewhat in the modern world, but less so in some places. When someone dies, the clocks at the time of death are stopped. All mirrors are covered over in the house where the deceased will be viewed. This keeps the spirit of the newly departed from being trapped in this world, unable to move on.

The women clear out a room where the deceased will be on display in the coffin. They clean, cook, and get everything ready for out-of-town family and friends arriving for the funeral. The men dig the grave and tidy up the graveyard. Throughout the days and nights during which the deceased is displayed, someone stays awake, keeping vigil with the dearly departed until burial takes place.

Leading up to the funeral, stories about the departed are told. There is laughter, and singing and prayers take place, and tears roll.

These wakes give the family and community strength and knit everyone closely together.

It is thought that a bird flying into a window foretells death; and death comes in threes.

The people of Southern Appalachia are very proud of their mixed ancestry. If you ask a Southern Appalachian, where he or she learnt to track and hunt, then you'll likely get a reply like, "From my Cherokee ancestors." Or you might hear them relate to their proud heritage in statements like, "See that beautiful stone building? My Italian ancestors built it. The Italians are some of the best stonecutters in the world." "Try some of our home-brew, it's just how my ancestors from Germany made it." You will hear someone say, "We preserve our vegetables as our family that came over from Cornwall, England, did." A voice swelling with pride states, "Our Irish ancestors taught us to make the best moonshine whiskey in these mountains."

There exists a quirky mixture of languages and regional pronunciation of words. *Tard* means tired. *Wasper* means wasp. *Brought up* refers to the place you were raised. A *booger* is a spook or monster, a *haint* a ghost or booger. *Boot* is something added to even up a sale or trade. *Bow up* is turning mean. *Beside oneself* refers to being disoriented. *Beholden to* means to be obligated or indebted to. A favorite of mine is the word *bumfuzzled*, being of a confused state of mind.

There are many reports of strange things people have seen, and an abundance of ghost stories. Tales of black panther sightings are common, as are those of seeing Bigfoot, shapeshifters, and of course, Mothman.

One of the most famous ghost stories of Southern Appalachia is that of Booger Mountain.

It is in Knox County, Kentucky, between the towns of Corbin and Barbourville on the old Route 25E.

There are several versions of the story, but most go something like the following: Back then, people were still crossing the mountain on horseback or in horse-drawn wagons. One day, a woman was killed on top of the mountain. No one ever found out who killed her.

She could not rest in peace, and late at night, when people were crossing the mountain, she rode on horseback or in the back of a wagon, looking for her killer. Hence the locale became known as Booger Mountain. As time passed and cars started traveling over the mountain, the ghost of the murdered woman appeared on the running board of older cars, or sometimes the fender. At the bottom of the mountain she would vanish.

As time passed, cars and trucks changed, but still to this day, drivers report seeing the ghost of this beautiful woman getting beside them or climbing into the back seat as they drive across it.

Several years ago, an old man told my grandfather that a young, beautiful woman was in fact killed on top of the mountain, and it is said that her boyfriend likely committed the crime; he was never identified or found.

For those with access to the spiritual world, she is still visible today, searching for the one who cut her young, precious life so short. Sadly, when tragic events like this occur, justice is seldom served.

During the U.S. Civil War, the Confederate Army would leave two soldiers on top of a huge rock on the mountain above the Little Shepherd Trail. From atop the rock, the Confederate soldiers were able to see a great distance across the valley to watch out for Union troops traveling the Hagan Trail.

One day, Union soldiers were spotted traveling across the trail. One of the rebels rode away to warn the Confederate Army.

The next morning, Union troops surrounded the rebel soldier atop the rock. They fought for two days before he was killed. The Union soldiers left his body lying at the base of the rock.

Locals living in the area buried the rebel soldier. His remains are still there today.

This huge rock has been known since as Rebel Rock. People traveling the Little Shepherd Trail in the early morning or late afternoon will often talk about seeing the rebel soldier standing atop the rock, keeping watch and never leaving his post.

In the 1930s, a little girl got off a bus after returning from church. Her dog, a white German Shepherd, was there waiting on her. As the two were walking home along the edge of the road, the bus went on toward the next stop. The dog ran out in front of it, and the little girl went after her dog. The bus ran both over, killing them instantly.

Since the death of the girl and her dog, a great number of people have reported seeing them walk along the road on which they got run over. A well-respected schoolteacher's car broke down near the spot. All houses nearby had been abandoned and torn down, and the area was very secluded. It was late at night, nearing dawn. At this hour, there was never much traffic on the road.

The schoolteacher was very afraid and trying to figure out what she should do. Suddenly, a little girl, dressed in white, with a white dog by her side, appeared at the driver-side window.

The little girl said, "Don't be afraid, Rex and I will stay with you until the coal miners on the hoot-owl shift come by. It won't be long."

A short while later she said, "I now see the lights of the miners coming down the mountain."

The schoolteacher looked at the lights, but when she turned back to the little girl and dog, they were both gone. She never saw either again.

During the U.S. Civil War, the people of Harlan County, Kentucky, were largely supporters of the Union. However, that changed in the spring of 1862. A 12-year-old mulatto boy took his family mule to the creek to be watered. A patrol of Union soldiers came by and wanted to take his mule. The young boy resisted. The Union troops took the mule and hung the 12-year-old boy by the reins from a paw-paw tree.

The young boy and his family were well-respected throughout the county, and this incident turned most of the people in the area against Union soldiers.

Potholes were dug out and only slightly covered over on the Hagan Trail near high cliffs. Often, as Union soldiers passed through, a sniper shot took the life of a poor soul; the ambushed men panicked, and the potholes crippled and killed two or three horses and as many soldiers.

At times in early spring, the young boy can be seen along the edge of the creek, looking for his mule.

Folktales such as these are as plentiful in Southern Appalachia as flees on the back of a stray dog, with each being unique, much like the people of the region.

Southern Appalachians

The freshness of the morning, sun coming up, dew rising. The warmth and beauty of the day, sunshine or rain. Southern Appalachians and their old mountain ways. The summer evenings, the smell of honeysuckle, the taste of blackberry pie, and the feel of a cool mountain breeze.

Love that bonds the devoted family, roots that run deep. The wandering spirit in some, but before journeys end will return, as for Southern Appalachians this is home, and where it all began; so is inherited a deep respect and connection to the past, sassafras tea, sweet southern charm.

Precious memories, keepsakes, and stories, pass from elders to descendants, like pictures from the family album found in the old dresser drawer. Our home, our childhood, special times, heartaches, the good times, and the bad. The past that traces for generations makes us who we are, Southern Appalachians.

A painted sky, and gradually the sun goes down in Southern Appalachia. The family gathers on the front porch, the day surrenders, the sky grows darker as we settle in for the night. The moon and stars fill the heavens, and we're watching the magical lights of fireflies and listen to the sounds of the night in Southern Appalachia.

Looking back with pleasure, remembering those evenings on the front porch and the sounds of the night, I value even more the simple life, what nature taught when the world was smaller, and I believed time would go on forever. I reflect on the peace of the moment with family past and present, and it warms me with awe, and deep respect of my roots, till my journey ends and I return, forever, to Southern Appalachia.

A Dog's Love

In the 1950s and 1960s, long before video games and smartphones, the children of Appalachia discovered many ways to play and amuse themselves. In the winter, there were snowball fights, and there was sledding and building snowmen. In the summer, they'd play up in the mountains, and along the streams and rivers. They'd swing on vines from trees, swim in the streams, and build homemade wagons to ride down the many hills.

One summer morning, Steve, Juanita, Lisa, and Chris, were tossing stones in the stream that flowed past their home. As always, Juanita's brown-and-white, mid-sized dog, Rusty, accompanied them. The children lived close to each other and attended the same school. They were always looking for adventures, especially during the summer break from school.

This summer morning, while skipping stones on the stream, Steve came up with an idea. "That old rusty car by the abandoned house has a nice top on it. If we get an old axe and hacksaw, we can cut it off and use it like a raft. We'll float all the way down to the river! We should cut four poles to push off. And to guide with. And when we reach the river, we just sink it and walk back home before dark."

It sounded like fun, and the children all agreed to it; in a very short time, they sawed off the top of the old car and placed it in the stream. Each child had a long pole to guide with.

Juanita's dog Rusty jumped into the makeshift raft while the children were already floating down the stream. He didn't like it, jumped out, and paddled to shore. He stayed with the children all the way, running along them, barking and playing.

As the raft neared the river, the water became deeper and swifter. The front of the car top dipped into the water, and sank within seconds, dumping the children into the stream.

Juanita, Chris, and Steve were swimming to reach the shore, when they noticed that something was wrong with Lisa. She was fighting fiercely to keep her head above the water.

The friends hasted to Lisa's aid. Her feet were tangled up in a heap of old fence wire, which had washed downstream, likely after heavy rain, when water running off the mountains had more than doubled the stream in volume. Rusty was on the shore barking, and suddenly ran off.

Nearby, Fred Seals, a mechanic, was at work in his auto repair shop. The door of his garage was up. Rusty stormed in, loudly barking, then turned and ran back toward the door. The dog did so three or four times before Fred realized that he wanted to be followed.

As Fred got outside, he heard the faint sound of children yelling for help. He picked up the pace to keep up with the running dog. A customer saw Fred running as she parked her car; she got out and followed too.

He reached the stream and saw two kids trying to hold a girl's head above the water, while another was going under, trying to free her from whatever was holding her. Fred waded in and was able to lift the girl and the fence wire up enough for the children to free her feet. The customer observed this and yelled out that she'd call for help.

On shore, Fred got a lot of the water out of Lisa's lungs. She was coughing and gagging, and almost unconscious. He picked her up and addressed her friends. "Dr. Davis' office is just a block away. Two of you go in the garage and call her family. Tell them where she'll be. One of you come with me in case he has any questions."

In his office, Dr. Davis checked that the water was out of Lisa's lungs, then took her vital signs and placed her on oxygen. He told his nurse to call for an ambulance to get her to hospital. Lisa's parents arrived a few minutes before the car.

Fred Seals told Lisa's parents to go to the hospital. "I'll take the children home. You stay with your daughter."

After five days in hospital, Lisa came home, but her road to recovery was far from over. Her speech wasn't much more than a grunt. She could understand things but could not talk very well. Her balance was so bad that she couldn't walk unassisted, or without a walker. The doctors didn't know whether her medical issues were physical, psychological, or both.

She had been home from hospital only a short time when her friends Juanita, Steve, and Chris, arrived for a visit. As always, Rusty was with them. Lisa sat on the couch, and he ran over and jumped up into her lap. From that moment on, the dog never left her side, day or night. He slept beside her, and if Lisa had a bad dream, woke her up. If she fell, his barking promptly alerted the family.

Her friends came to visit every day, and she was always pleased to see them, as was Rusty.

After one visit, Juanita said to Chris and Steve, "Somehow Rusty knew that Lisa needed him more than me. Now he is her dog."

Within ten months, Lisa was walking and talking, and back to her normal self. Her parents often said, "We think that the dog's love has done more for our daughter than all the doctors we took her to see."

Love is a powerful emotion, even a dog's love.

Redemption

Oscar Reeves grew up near London, Kentucky, in the foothills of the Appalachian Mountains. He came from a wealthy and politically connected family. Being the only child, Oscar inherited his family's wealth, which included several businesses and two large farms. He also had wealthy relatives in the area. Overall, he was part of a very powerful family.

Oscar's parents never let him have any pets other than a small fish tank with a few goldfish. As he grew older, and just like his parents before him, his dislike for dogs and cats grew stronger. He set out poison to try and kill any dogs or cats straying onto his land. He kept a .22 rifle handy to shoot any such animal spotted on his property. It was very common for people to let pets roam free, and many were lost while on Oscar's land.

Across the road from his home was a scattered community of working-class families, whom the young man disliked almost as much as their pets. Unscrupulous residents of that neighorhood set out to abandon unwanted pets, leaving them to survive on their own. Many times, they'd die on the roadway or by Oscar's hand. Sometimes they were picked up, taken into animal shelters, and the lucky ones were adopted into loving families.

Ed and Nan Coble along with their son Howard were a very happy family, who had recently moved into the community across from Oscar's land. When the Cobles moved in, they brought with them Howard's brown-and-white shelter dog, Socks. The day after they'd moved in, their neighbor Joyce came over to welcome them to the community. She warned them in no uncertain terms to keep their dog away from Oscar's farm. Joyce said, "When I first moved here, I had two German Shepherds, Rex and Bear. Oscar ran his farm truck off the edge of the road and killed Rex. Later, Bear walked across the end of his driveway, where Oscar shot and killed him. An elderly couple two houses down the road from mine had four cats. Oscar poisoned their grey-and-black cat as well as their yellow-and-white one. He ran over the first one with his truck while the other just disappeared. I'm sure he killed it too."

Joyce took a deep breath and went into more gruesome detail, "A little girl who used to live here had three kittens – a white one, a calico cat, and a yellow-white one. Oscar Reeves killed all three. And that's just what I got to know about since moving here six months ago."

Ed turned to Howard and said, "Okay, son, you heard what Joyce said. Be sure to keep Socks away from Mr. Reeves property."

Howard replied, "I'll watch out for him as best I can." The thought of his beloved companion running into this kind of peril made him furious and anxious all at once.

Ed was a long-haul truck driver. He was mostly home on weekends, and with Howard being an only child, his father knew how important Socks was to his son.

Life was going well for the Coble family. Winter and spring had come and gone. Howard made many friends in the community, who together were enjoying the summer. On one lovely day, he played frisbee with his friends. Socks too loved the game, yapping and snapping at the flying disc. The boys sailed the airborne frisbee on the winds and Socks ran to catch it. One boy flung it a little hard. It caught perfectly in a gust and sailed across the road, landing on the property of Oscar Reeves.

Oscar had already had his .22 rifle out that morning, shooting birds behind his house. He saw Socks running for the frisbee and quickly took aim and fired. Socks yelped when the bullet struck him. Crying out in pain, the dog ran behind bushes, where he fell out of sight. Hearing Socks yelp in pain, and without hesitation, Howard ran across the road toward the anguished sound. Oscar could no longer see Socks behind the bushes, but could hear him yelping, so he fired three more shots in the hope of finishing the dog off. Now

Oscar heard a boy yelling at him; he then saw two boys standing on the edge of the road, pointing behind the bushes. One boy turned and ran toward Howard's house to alert his mother. The other boy was afraid to go onto his property and kept pointing and yelling.

He figured the boy was just going on about the dog he had shot. He also noticed the dog wasn't yelping any longer. As he walked around the bushes, he saw it lying dead on the ground; behind the dog, a young boy lay on the floor, bleeding from his left temple. Without a sting of guilt, he assumed the boy was dead too. He immediately went into his house to call the local sheriff to conduct the investigation; he had recently helped put him in office. Oscar never offered any aid to the boy. He simply remained in the house, waiting for the sheriff and the ambulance to arrive.

Nan, Howard's mother, ran toward him, and quickly placed a towel on the wound to his head. Several other people ran over to the wounded boy to offer assistance. The people of the community were outraged that Oscar had shot Howard and killed his dog.

When the sheriff and ambulance arrived, they found Howard still alive. He was brought to the only hospital in the small town. From there, he was transported to a bigger facility in Lexington, Kentucky. Howard's mother never left his side. His friends took Socks and buried him on the back part of the Coble property.

Oscar walked up close to the sheriff and said, "That boy and his dog had no business being on my property. I didn't see the boy behind the bushes when I was shooting at the dog."

The sheriff said, "Oscar, it was just an accident. Don't worry, I will take care of it." This area is known throughout the state and adjoining states for its corruption. The wealthy, wielding political influence, can do as they please and get a pass from corrupt local politicians; thus, no charges were filed against Oscar Reeves for shooting Howard. Both sheriff and the district attorney deemed the shooting of the boy an accident, and as far as the law was concerned, it was over and done with. However, Howard's father, a Christian man, had to talk himself out of striking back at Oscar on many occasions.

After spending several weeks in hospital, Howard was released. He had lost his left eye; at first, the doctors thought he might lose his right one too, but when the swelling went down, he kept sight in it. He seemed to grieve the loss of his dog more than that of his eye.

Summer was coming to an end, and Howard was getting off the school bus. As it was driving away, and the children were walking home, he noticed a car passing by. It came to a halt just past the bus stop. The person sitting on the right side set a small dog out by the roadside, then drove away. The little dog chased after the vehicle, but in seconds it was going far too fast for it to keep up. After giving up the chase, it sat by the side of the road for a few minutes and then noticed Howard looking on. It ran and followed him home.

Howard sat on the front porch steps, when it ran up to him, wagging its tail, looking up to him as if to say, *I want to be your friend.* The tiny dog weighed twelve pounds and was a female. She was black with a few splashes of brown and white around her face and chest. She had pointed ears with long black hairs and sported a little growth at the edge of her left eye, which made the boy feel even more connected to her.

He took the dog inside and explained to his mother how she came to be here. "Mom, can I keep her please? She's so cute," he begged. Seeing how excited he was, she quickly agreed. They gave the little dog her first bath, then got her food and water. Nan told her son, "We'll take her to the vet tomorrow. Have you decided what you are going to name her?"

Howard replied, "I've been calling her Little Lady, and she seems to like it." Over the following months, Little Lady became a much-loved member of the Coble family, and just what Howard needed to start enjoying life again.

As the children were playing outside in the following spring, Little Lady suddenly ran to the edge of the road, barking toward the Reeves property. She ran back toward Howard, still barking, then across the road, and finally onto Oscar Reeves' land. Worried that he'd hurt or even kill Little Lady, the boy chased after her without concern for himself.

He ran toward the barking sound and found Oscar pined from the waist down beneath his farm tractor. He was groaning in pain. Howard said, "I'll run and get help."

Several people from the community ran over to help Oscar, while Howard's mother called the rescue squad and fire department. By the time they got him unstuck, he was unconscious. After five weeks in hospital, he had recovered enough to return home. While in hospital, Oscar couldn't help but think of the dog and little boy who had saved him – the same boy who he'd shot, causing him to go blind in his left eye, and killing his dear dog. The words of a nurse at the hospital haunted him. She had said, "Mr. Reeves, while you were sedated, a young boy came to see you. He had a patch over his left eye. He sat with you a long time, and left you flowers before he left."

The choking sensation of guilt made him call Pastor Webb. When the pastor arrived at his hospital bed, Oscar's voice was broken and full of remorse. "Most of my life I attended church services only because I thought it was expected of me. I've been a miserable and hateful man. I've caused much pain and suffering, been cruel in many ways. Yet being near death has opened my eyes. I want to live the rest of my life as a better man, a better human being. I can never make up for all the hurt I have caused, but I'll do all I can to right my many wrongs."

Pastor Webb prayed with Oscar. "Ask God for forgiveness, seek forgiveness from those you've wronged, and finally, learn to forgive yourself."

When Oscar got home, he cleaned up and went across the road to the Coble home. He was invited in and entered with his head down. Once he'd gathered the inner strength, he looked up and started by thanking Howard and his little dog for saving his life. He looked the boy in the eye and begged his forgiveness for what he had done to him. Howard and his family accepted his plea and expressed their forgiveness. A moved Oscar declared, "I have a few plans I would like to share with you. First, I want to pay all of Howard's medical bills, past and future. If there is a way to get him a new eye, I will find it. Pastor Webb told me that he wants to be a veterinarian. I will set up a full scholarship for him. I'm going to give $100,000 to the county animal shelter, to help upgrade and maintain their facility. I'm going to build another animal shelter on my property to handle the overflow. And Howard, if you don't mind, I have a lot of land you and your friends and pets can explore and play on."

Howard smiled. "What will you name the new animal shelter?"

"How about, *Socks' and Little Lady's No Kill Animal Shelter*," suggested Oscar.

"That sounds great."

For the next fifteen years, Howard and Oscar worked together and became close friends. Howard became a veterinarian, opening an animal hospital next to the shelter. When Oscar died from a heart attack, he left all his property and holdings to him, along with a short note which read, *'Thank you for forgiving me, and for your friendship. Thank you for helping me become a better person. I know you will use what I leave behind to help make the world a better place. Your most loyal and devoted friend, Oscar Reeves.'*

Herb and His Banjo

The first licensed radio broadcasting began on August 20, 1920. Herbert Helton - Herb, as he was called - was nine-years-old at the time. He grew up attending services at the local Baptist Church on Sundays. He enjoyed hearing the ministers preach, learning about the Bible and the holy word; but what Herb liked most was the gospel music. He wasn't a great singer, but he loved to sing.

Herb was the son of John D. Helton and Mary Brock. Herb Helton's grandfather Paul had been born a slave in the Cherokee Nation of Oklahoma in 1861. Paul's father was of Black African- and Cherokee heritage, and considered a slave, and his mother a Black African slave. Paul was born into slavery. However, at the end of the U.S. Civil War it was decided that all slaves within the Cherokee Nation would become enrolled members of the Cherokee Nation known as Freedmen, or Cherokee Freedmen. At four years of age, Paul became an enrolled member of the Cherokee Nation.

In time, Paul fathered five sons and three daughters by two different women, with John D. being his youngest son. In his late teens, John D. took a job for a railroad company, helping to lay new tracks. He found his way to Kentucky through his work.

In Knott County, John met and married Mary Brock. It may not have been love at first sight, but it was very close to it. Mary had mixed African slave ancestry from Virginia, and Cherokee English roots from Kentucky.

After John and Mary were married, he stopped working on the railroads and took a fresh job with a local logging company. He was not well-educated, but he could read and write in both English and the Cherokee language. Mary only had an elementary education.

After two years with the logging company, John bought a small farm in Knott County, and he cultivated it well. The couple had six children, of whom Herb was the oldest. They attended school and went to church on Sundays with their parents. John and Mary read to them from the Bible each night. The Heltons were well-liked and respected in their community, and all their children well-mannered.

One afternoon, Herb strolled past a local mining company store. Company stores paid their workers in company script, which meant they could only spend it in the store. He heard a man playing a banjo on the store's porch and was instantly fascinated with the sound of the instrument.

He stayed and listened until the man stopped playing. Later in life he often said, "That was the most beautiful sound I'd ever heard. It changed my life."

Herb paid a visit to Old Man Taylor, who was known for picking up things from here and there, and good at making things. He told him about the wonderful music the man was making on the banjo. Old Man Taylor said, "I've seen and heard the banjo many times. It's a wonderful instrument."

Herb asked, "Can you help me make a banjo? It's exactly the kind of music I want to make."

"Sure, I have made two banjos before, but never learned to play one. You might be interested to know that the instrument was brought to the United States during the slave trade from West Africa, where it was called a *bania*. It's a stringed instrument of the lute family, with a round body, and a long wooden neck," explained knowledgeable Old Man Taylor.

For the next three weeks, Herb and the old man worked at making a banjo. They used a round tin pan with a hickory wood neck. Herb carved the keys from white oak with his Case XX pocketknife. Old Man Taylor got Herb an old set of strings. Now the boy finally learned to play the wondrous instrument; anytime he wasn't in school, church, or working with his dad, he strummed on his banjo. Over the next two years, he had taught himself to make wonderful music with his homemade instrument. One afternoon he was sitting on the edge of a railroad bridge crossing the river. His shoeless feet swung above the water to the rhythm of his music. Revered Wilson came walking down the tracks. He heard the pretty music the young boy was producing. He thought to himself, 'That kid can really play.'

He asked, "Young man, where did you get your banjo, and who taught you to play it?"

The boy replied, "Old Man Taylor helped me make it, and as for playing, I've just been teaching myself."

"What's your name, boy?"

"Herb Helton, Sir."

The Reverend said, "Well, Herb Helton, why don't you follow me down to the church. I have something I would like to give you. Deacon Miller lost his wife five years ago. He's a grouchy old cuss, but with a good heart. He just cares to hide it. After his wife passed away, he donated a lot of her things to the church. Amongst the items is an old banjo. It has been gathering dust in the backroom of the church, waiting for a new home. And I believe it has now found one with you. When we get down to the church, it is yours. I only ask you to come by every now and then on Sundays to play your pretty music for us."

"Yes Sir, I will, I surely will," replied Herb, overjoyed.

After getting hold of the new banjo, there was no stopping him. He slowly perfected his skills, and his music was echoing throughout the hills and mountains of Southern Appalachia. Herb played for different churches, black, mixed, and white. He performed at social events. Mining companies paid him to perform at company stores to entertain both customers and workers.

It wasn't long before the young musician began traveling with a tent revival church throughout Kentucky and neighboring states. No matter where he played, he always promoted God, Kentucky, and Southern Appalachia, through his music.

At the time, radio was becoming popular, and stations began to pop up all over the nation. In the later part of the 1920s, several stations had contacted Reverend Wilson about getting Herb to perform live on their broadcasts. When the reverend spoke to Herb about it, he quickly agreed. He soon got used to being introduced by the director of a broadcast, then later ending a program with his music. It wasn't long until the name Herb Helton was synonymous with banjo music throughout the region.

In his native Southern Appalachia, everyone knew that Herb was a negro, but sadly in other areas of the country, people did not. In the last part of the 1920s, the popular musician gave a live interview at a radio station in Louisville, Kentucky.

The program director said, "Ladies and gentlemen, the beautiful banjo playing you just heard was performed by Herb Helton. Herb, where are you from?"

"I'm from Knott County, Kentucky. I was born and raised there, and all my family still live there," answered the guest.

"Herb, are you the first…or at least… one of the first negroes to perform on live radio? I'm sure you are proud of that."

"Well, yes Sir, I am very proud of it."

"I've heard you also have Cherokee blood?"

"Yes, Sir, I do have some Cherokee blood, and a mix of others. We are who we are. The Good Lord makes us the way He wants us so we can serve His will."

The program director asked, "So you are a God-fearing man, Herb?"

"Oh yes, Sir, I surely am. With God, all things are possible."

The interviewer probed further, "Herb, do you believe being a negro has helped, or hurt, your great success?"

Herb inhaled deeply, to give himself time to formulate a thoughtful reply, "Sir, I don't think folks much care what color the person is who's making the music. When people hear pretty music, it soothes the heart and soul. It inspires and encourages them, and that's what matters most. The Good Lord gave us music to bring us closer together and to put smiles on our faces. Nothing makes me happier than playing my banjo and seeing people smile."

"Herb, thank you for performing for us today, and taking the time to talk with us. Your music and faith are an inspiration to us all. Now if you will, please play one more song to close our program."

Family

Shillalah and Crockett Stevens, along with their four children, were headed south in their small RV on Interstate 75 in Kentucky. They were returning to North Carolina from taking the children on vacation to the Cedar Point Amusement Park on the shore of Lake Eerie, near Sandusky, Ohio. After passing two trucks, Shillalah saw the blue lights of a police car in the mirror. She looked down at the speedometer. She was going ten miles per hour over the limit.

After she pulled the RV over on the shoulder of the road, a deputy sheriff approached on the driver's side and said, "I clocked you at eleven miles over the limit. I need your driver's license and proof of insurance."

The deputy wrote her a ticket and told her, "You can mail this in at the address at the bottom or go by the sheriff's department and pay it."

Shillalah got directions from the officer. She drove to the address. Her seven-year-old son Bo and six-year-old daughter Myra went in to watch their mother pay the ticket; three-year-old Linda and four-year-old Zac remained in the car with their father.

An hour before issuing Shillalah's speeding ticket, deputies had responded to reports of a man standing on a high bridge, contemplating jumping off. He was standing still, staring at a shiny penny in his hand. One of the officers asked, "Are you okay?"

The man holding the penny replied, "I was ready to jump. Then I saw this shiny penny on the pavement and picked it up and read the words *In God We Trust* …and feel that everything is going to be okay."

The deputy said he'd take the man to the sheriff's department to figure out what to do and where to get him help.

Shillalah and her children entered the doorway of the sheriff's office. They saw a man sitting and waiting. He was in his mid-thirties, of average size, with dark hair, wearing jeans, a black t-shirt, and a denim jacket. He looked confused and lost, but still managed to smile at them. The children took a seat as their mother went to pay her ticket at the counter. The woman behind the counter talked audibly about the man waiting by the door. She said, "Poor thing, when they found him, it looked like he'd been beaten and hit by a car. He was near death and in hospital for six weeks. He doesn't know his name or where he's from. Nothing came back on his fingerprints or DNA. Looks like he's lost to the world."

Shillalah got her turn at the counter. Once she'd paid, she overheard a call on the police radio. Several people were fighting in the courtroom. Two women and one male deputy ran out of the office.

As she turned to leave, her children were talking to the man by the door. At that moment, something extraordinary happened. She had a brief vision in which she heard the voice of the Creator telling her to take the man with them. The last time Shillalah had such a powerful vision was when her husband Crockett lost both of his legs from his knees down in an RPG attack while serving in the Army in Iraq.

As she approached her children and the man, she looked into his eyes and asked sincerely, "Do you want to come with us?"

He replied, answering both her words and hypnotic gaze, "Well, thanks. I'm not sure why…something inside is telling me I should. Yes, thank you. I will go with you."

Within ten minutes, the RV was back on the highway heading home. Shillalah whispered to her husband about her vision and what she'd overheard the woman say about the man. Crockett turned to him and said, "Welcome to the family. Since you don't remember your name, what would you like to be known as?"

He looked very lost again. "There is nothing I can think of." He told the family how he'd felt since getting out of hospital, and about standing on the bridge and finding the shiny penny. Crockett was himself lost in thought for a moment, then replied, "My grandfather was from Harlan County, Kentucky, so how about we call you Harlan Stevens…my cousin from Cawood, Kentucky? How does that sound?"

The man smiled, which cleared the confusion off his features. "Harlan Stevens, yeah, that sounds just fine…but why are you folks so willing to help me?"

Crockett said, "No one who knows my wife would ever question one of her visions. We always try to help people in need where we can."

Seven-year-old Bo put his hand out to the stranger. "Hello Harlan, it's very nice to meet you." The other children did the same, giving newly-named Harlan an odd yet warm sense of belonging. Shillalah already thought about practicalities, and added, "I have a cousin who will help you get a driver's license and social security number." Her husband added, "We live on a small farm near Birdtown, North Carolina. My uncle Luc lives with us and helps manage the farm, which we are grateful for since I am limited in the work I can do. We count twenty-eight head of Black Angus cattle, nineteen hogs, four horses, and far too many chickens to count. Our old family home is getting run down. We are in the slow process of building a new, larger one. We want to grow our family." Crockett glanced lovingly at Shillalah. "I get a medical retirement from the Army. My wife and the children are enrolled members of the Eastern Band of Cherokee and get a small annuity payment from the tribe. She also teaches at the local school. We are far from rich, Harlan, but we get by okay and live a blessed life among family and friends."

Shillalah was driving, and her husband and the kids were sat at the table in the back of the RV, talking to their new friend. Nosey Myra asked what music he liked. Harlan replied, "I really don't know. For the most part, my entire past is a blank." The chattering children wanted to know the type of books, movies, and food, Harlan liked. Most of that he couldn't remember. Yet a single car journey later, he already felt like a long-lost family member to the Stevens.

As it was getting dark, the family reached their home. Uncle Luc took to Harlan right off, but waited for the next day to hear how he came to be there. The new family member slept on the couch during the first night. The next day, the apartment above the garage was cleaned up for him; it was a nice space, around one hundred feet from the main house.

Everyone needs a purpose in life, and Harlan found his in farm life – helping with the gardens, tending to livestock, and working on the new house. He developed a sense of family and found his place in the world through the simple affection and kindness offered by strangers. He was quick to help others and just as fast at making friends. Yet his secret stayed within the Stevens family.

Three years had passed in this blissful manner. Harlan and the family were gathered in the living room of the old house on Christmas morning. He had a girlfriend now by the name of Karen, who'd joined for the celebrations. Holiday music was playing as everyone watched the children open their gifts.

Harlan was overwhelmed by the powerful sense of bonding and belonging within the family, as so often during festive gatherings. "Thank you all for the gifts…and I'd like to add how happy I am to be here with everyone I love so much. I am truly a blessed man."

Shillalah said, "We all love you, Harlan, and are just as blessed to have you as part of our family. We should all feel blessed if next year we get to have Christmas in the new house." Everyone cheered and agreed.

One summer afternoon, Harlan, Crockett, and Shillalah were sitting together on the front porch. Crockett looked over the gorgeous landscape and remarked, "That sure is a beautiful sunset."

"It sure is," nodded Harlan very slowly, as if repeating with words the almost invisible sneak of the sun below the horizon, "and I have to say, it brings about a wonderful feeling of peace and a sense of something greater."

Crockett sensed it intensely…the entire meaning of life harbored within the plethora of sunset tones. "It sure does, but it wasn't always like that for me. I used to like to get a little hurly-burly. Then I joined the Army and married my beautiful wife, and all changed for me. I discovered the meaning of happiness."

Shillalah cuddled her husband, seeking his warmth, and sharing hers. "I've always heard that life is like an echo, you get back what you send out."

Harlan replied, "I do agree with that, but I've also learned that no matter how bad things seem today, life goes on and can be better tomorrow. It is a slow process to learn to take full responsibility for who we want to be. Then, with a bit of luck, the glow of a greater life begins to shine through."

"Well said, dear Harlan. You have a lovely way with words," said Shillalah.

Three weeks later, a severe thunderstorm hit the area. Just after midnight, the old farmhouse was hit by lightning. The electricity went out, flashed back on, then cut out again. Crockett awoke to the smell of smoke. He shook Shillalah awake and put on his prostheses. Uncle Luc came in from the back bedroom. The house was already aflame. Luc and Shillalah stormed up the stairs. He grabbed Bo and Myra and took them downstairs, out the front door. He raced back upstairs and found Shillalah in the hallway, coughing, overtaken by thick, almost impenetrable, smoke. As he helped her downstairs, Crockett was there to get her outside.

Harlan heard the thunder. He looked out of the apartment window and witnessed the flames shooting from the house. He ran to help as quickly as his legs carried him. As Crockett and Luc got Shillalah out, Harlan reached them. Luc, in a very sharp voice, informed him that Zac and Linda were still upstairs.

Harlan ran through the smoke and flames almost completely blind. He sprinted up the stairs. The two children hovered by the back bedroom window, clutching their cat. It was a stray who they'd given a new home to. Harlan pulled a sheet from the bed and ripped it into three pieces, which he tied together. He wrapped it around Linda and lowered her almost to the ground before having to let go of it. He told her to run and get help. He fetched a second sheet and did the same with Zac, who still clawed into his cat while Harlan lowered him to safety. By now, the burning roof collapsed in on him. His clothes shot up in flames. He pulled himself toward the window…threw himself out of it with last resolve…and dropped to the ground like dead weight.

Crockett reached him first and smothered his burning clothes. Luc, as weak as he was, helped Crockett drag Harlan, Shillalah, and the children, well away from the blazing inferno. The sounds of sirens from the fire department and EMTs wailed in the distance. Shillalah was back on her feet, checking on her little ones. Crockett fetched a blanket from the truck and placed it over Harlan. The rain was coming down with very little effect on the burning house.

As the EMTs ran to Harlan, he opened his eyes a little. As if from a distance, he heard Crockett whisper, "Thank you for saving our children." He replied in a very weak voice, "I love each and every one of you. Your love is truly heaven-sent. Thank you for being my family."

He closed his eyes, and the EMTs loaded him into the ambulance. Luc stayed behind to see on things on the farm, while Crockett and Shillalah and the children followed in the car to the hospital.

Mother and children were unscathed, apart from having taken in smoke. Uncle Luc arrived a few hours later in need of oxygen. After four hours of waiting, the doctor came out and informed the family that the team had done all they could to save him. "I'm sorry. He passed away due to his injuries." The entire family was in tears, everyone tightly holding one another for comfort.

The old house was almost a total loss. The new house was near-ready, and the family moved in a little earlier than planned. They were now as lost without Harlan as he'd been years ago when he was freshly released from hospital.

Shillalah went into his apartment. There were pictures of all the family on his walls. By his bed was a Bible and a Cherokee medicine bag; on top of the Bible was the shiny penny he'd found on the bridge the day he had thought about jumping. She read the words on the penny out loud, "In God We Trust," then slotted the coin into her pocket. Later, she showed it to her husband. "I want this penny placed in his pocket and buried with him."

After the funeral and burial in the family graveyard, the Stevens gathered around Harlan's grave. Uncle Luc remarked that they never got to know who he really was.

Shillalah replied, "In life, we have family by blood and family by choice. He loved us and we loved him, and he gave his life to save our children. He was a kind man full of love for us. He used to say that kindness is a language the deaf can hear and the blind can see. Who he really was is exactly who he was meant to be. Our family.

Strong Medicine

For many generations, the Cherokee village in the green valley below the Mountain of Eagles thrived, and its people were happy. Gradually, this thriving and happy village changed; its people became selfish, greedy, loud and disrespectful. The ones that had most, were exerting control over those with less. In such a way they lived without honoring the Creator and themselves.

After several discussions, the Council of Elders decided to place a man high upon the Mountain of Eagles to watch the people of the village, identify the issues, and find a way to correct them. This man was to spend one full year observing from the peak of the mountain. Food and supplies would be provided daily. The names of many suitable warriors were talked about. Yet most of the young men wanted to hunt and train to be warriors, and either had a wife, or were looking for one.

One Elder spoke up, "We are looking in the wrong direction. Most of our young men have no desire to spend a whole year on the mountain alone. However, there is a woman called Looks-at-Clouds. Two summers ago, she followed her husband, Red Bear, to war in the North, where she fought by his side; when he fell in battle, she continued to fight bravely, helping to finally turn the events into victory. She has said that she will take no other husband. Looks-at-Clouds spends days hunting on her own. She is as good with the bow and spear as the men of the village. This assignment will be good for her and for our people."

So it was decided - the Council of Elders asked Looks-at-Clouds to spend a year on the Mountain of Eagles to make observations in order to learn how to help the people of the village thrive and be happy again. She agreed to the task, for the sake of her people. Supplies were taken to the top of the mountain, and a small structure was built for her to live in.

The designee took her task very seriously. She watched and she learned. Many of the things she saw saddened her, while others seemed petty and insignificant. Other than her people, she also got to observe wildlife and trees as the seasons came and went.

Each night, villagers witnessed the meager fire above of Looks-at-Clouds; on the night of the seventh new moon, her small fire turned into a huge bonfire, and images swirled around the flames. Thunder roared and lightning flashed from above the mountain, but not a drop of rain fell. This spectacle continued for seven nights. The Medicine Man told the villagers that the Creator had sent the Gods from the Sky Vault to counsel Looks-at-Clouds.

As the year came to an end, Looks-at-Clouds walked down from the mountain. She was dressed in all-white buckskin, adorned with beautiful beads and shells. Her hair was long and dark as the night, held in place firmly with a white headband. She looked as fresh as a spring morning.

The wise warrior was taken to the center of the village for everyone to hear her message. She started by saying, "I am no longer looking down on you from the mountain, but I assure you that the Creator and Gods in the Sky Vault are always looking upon us. They are there when we need them most." Addressing an ever-growing number of villagers, she raised her voice like a wave increasing in size under a strong wind, "In the past year, I saw from this village some good, a lot of bad, and a considerable amount in between. I have witnessed births, deaths, hunger, neglect, infidelity, a few smiles and many tears. Please remember, life is a journey, not a destination. Our experiences aren't measured by the number of days we live, or the number of breaths we take, but by how we grow above our limitations through love. Life and love are our prime gifts. Let's learn once more to embrace and celebrate all aspects of life, and pay attention to the simple, small things. Spend as much time as you can with your loved ones, and always remember that they are not among us forever."

She continued to address the villagers, who were in awe of the wisdom of her words and her clear, hypnotic voice. "One lovely summer's day, an elderly couple brought me a basket of food up to the mountain. They looked over the valley below and commented on the beauty of the day, and how they wished they could have more days exactly like this one. A short time later, I saw two children play in a field. They were having a wonderful time, never concerned with yesterday or tomorrow. By contrast, the elderly couple didn't fully enjoy the day as they were preoccupied with clinging to it. Live life for today by letting go of everything else, and let the mistakes of yesterday fade from memory."

Other than her mouth moving, Looks-at-Clouds was perfectly still, as if the Gods had imbued her with the majesty of a monument. "When the leaves turn green in the early spring, we are blessed with the feeling of freshness and the renewal of the circle of life. In the summer, the same leaves shade us from the heat of the sun. In the autumn, they paint the forest and mountains in vibrant colors, thus warning us of the coming of winter. At last, the time comes for the leaves to float and swirl to the ground. These same leaves provide food for many forms of life, as well as supplying food back to our nurturing Mother Earth to suckle the trees and plants in the coming spring. All life travels in a circle. And yes, there are things that happen which we struggle to accept. We lose people closest to us, and sadness takes over our hearts. In time, we learn to let go. Overcoming these events is part of the circle of life and gives us dignity."

Through her act of talking, Looks-at-Clouds began to renew the villagers' sense of wonder. "Any of us who have watched squirrels know they store the food they need to carry them through the harshness of winter. The deer on the other hand, although gentle and peaceful, alert us to danger instantly. Wildlife and forest are our greatest teachers. Through them, we remain open and willing to learn. Watch the geese, watch how they fly in V-formation; with the leader out front, they share a common direction and sense of community. Only together are they able get to where they are going. Travel is easier in formation. Notice how when the lead goose gets tired, it rotates back, making room for another goose to lead. We learn that it is good to take turns doing hard jobs, and to take the lead every now and then. The geese at the back honk to encourage the leader and those up front to keep going. It is wise to encourage our leaders, or else make criticism positive and constructive rather than destructive. When a goose gets sick or injured and falls out of formation, a few geese always follow it down for protection, and stay with it until it is either able to fly, or dies. Only then will they launch out on their own. It is important to be willing to stand by others and help."

"As I was watching from the mountain, I first thought that some of the problems below were petty and insignificant. It is easy to detect problems from afar, but harder to know the severity until we have traveled the same path and dealt with the same issues as those on the experiencing side. I learnt that there are no insignificant troubles. I encourage you to always seek counsel with family, friends, or tribal elders, and not regard any problem as too insignificant to address. We have all experienced hurt in our lives. We've felt bitterness, resentment, and hatred. Negative energy is a heavy burden to carry and can swallow us up with pain and guilt. A wise person acknowledges the pain in order to let it go. A mature person is kind and thankful and appreciates life as a gift. He or she does not take anything for granted. When we look east in the morning and thank the Creator for the new day, we should say it with a pure heart. Train yourselves to be patient and unselfish. Respect means acknowledging boundaries. We respect ourselves when we don't let people push us around. When we give our time or possessions of our own free will, it feels right and is healthy; but when others attempt to manipulate us, we need to respect ourselves enough to say *no*. Conversely, show respect to others by not using guilt or bullying as a means of control. And never be too afraid or ashamed to stand up for someone who is small, alone, and unable to stand up for himself or herself."

"We are wise to let others make their own choices without our interference. That doesn't mean we have to agree with them entirely, or follow their example. But it means that we value their individuality. We all have difficult choices to make in our lives. None of our families are perfect. We look on dreams that were crushed, or have not yet come to be fulfilled. Still, we continue to work hard and make the best of our abilities, so we can contribute to our families, clan, and tribe. Growing old is inevitable, yet maturity is optional. We don't get wiser by merely living longer. We make choices as people to grow wiser and more mature."

"Maturity prepares us for the harshness of cold winds, and dry times, and events unknown. How we act in harsh times defines how we will come to be known, not how many possessions we have. Always love and honor the Creator, in everything you do. Honor your family, tribe, and all others; remain dedicated to your faith day and night for your entire life."

"Where I stand today, a large white pole will be put in place, with a white buckskin flag waving at the top. It will remind you of the purity and faith in your hearts. Each person, young and old, should touch the pole every morning before going to the water."

By the time Looks-at-Clouds finished speaking, four days had passed. When the sun came up, she strode to the center of the village and spoke again until it went down. At the end of the day, the white pole with the white flag was put in place. No one detected any sign of tiredness or hunger on Looks-at-Cloud's face. After her almost weeklong speech, she still looked as fresh as a glorious spring day.

Her time on the mountain had helped to make her village prosperous and happy once again. She soon traveled to other Cherokee towns and villages to share her knowledge and wisdom with all those willing to listen. She became known as *Looks-at-Clouds, Beloved Woman with Strong Medicine*. Neighboring tribes invited the now famous warrior to speak, including the tribe that took the life of her husband.

Still to this day, the voice and wisdom of Looks-at-Clouds echoes from atop the Mountain of Eagles.

Keeper of Stories

Since creation, and long before Cherokee teacher and scholar Sequoyah (1773 – 1843) invented the Cherokee syllabary, making many of the Cherokee people literate in a very short time, storytelling had always served as a means to preserve the history and culture of the Cherokee.

The story of one such great orator has been told for many generations. When he was at the age of two summers, a rockslide took the life of his father, injured his mother, and crushed his legs. As he recovered and grew, he was able to stand on his left leg, but his right one never again supported him without the aid of a crutch. His mother, Little Dove, cared for his every need. He took the name of Lame Dove, for both his mother and his cripped leg. In later years, his name changed, as was common in Cherokee tradition.

The people, including the children of his village, were kind to him. It was, however, heart-breaking to his mother to witness him try so hard to play with the other children. A young boy named Traveling Wolf, who was six summers of age, paid a great deal of attention to Lame Dove; over time, they became close friends. Sometimes, Traveling Wolf helped him walk to the field to watch the men and boys play stickball; at other times, he carried him on his shoulders to a huge rock overlooking the river, to catch the breath-taking view. Here, they often sat together and watched the sunset. It reminded them to reach the village before the fall of darkness.

As the years passed, the friendship of the two boys grew stronger, and it became very clear to Traveling Wolf and the people of the village just how intelligent his friend was. He remembered in vivid detail the things he saw, and easily recalled conversations he had had or overheard. Sometimes, Traveling Wolf took Lame Dove down to the river to fish or to play in the shallows. Lame Dove could swim a little, but due to his crippled leg, could not be left unattended. His uncle made him a small bow and arrow, one that he could shoot from his knees or in a sitting position. Traveling Wolf spent many hours teaching Lame Dove to shoot.

After several years, Little Dove took another husband. As per tradition, women married outside of their own clan, and always owned the home, including all belongings; they had total control of the children. A Cherokee woman could divorce her husband any time she so desired. Lame Dove's new father was called Muskrat. He was a great warrior and hunter. He provided well for his family and was very affectionate toward the boy.

What Lame Dove looked forward to most was spending time with his friend, Traveling Wolf. He sat, patiently waiting, for him to come by.

As Traveling Wolf grew older, the boys spent more time with the men, learning to hunt, training to be warriors. He often felt guilty walking past his friend and merely exchanging a few kind words. At times, his guilt took over and he walked the long way around the village, so that he'd not have to pass by his friend at all; yet still, Lame Dove kept sitting patiently each day in the hope that Traveling Wolf would come.

When the guilt got too much, he visited Lame Dove. No matter how long it had been, his friend was always full of joy at seeing him. When he tried to explain why he hadn't come by, Lame Dove told him it was fine, that he understood. When he was twelve summers of age, Traveling Wolf noticed how children gathered around his friend to hear his stories. At night, many of the adults as well as some of the elders who he'd learned the stories from, flocked around him to listen attentively.

Lame Dove's voice was clear, sincere, and carried deep feeling; he added excitement or sadness to his tales as the mood called for. Much like a modern-day filmmaker, Lame Dove had the ability to make people feel as if they were being part of the action, right at the center of the event he was talking about. It was during this time that the people of his village started calling him Keeper of Stories, no longer referring to his older name.

Keeper of Stories not only knew the history and culture of his people; he was as good at understanding and predicting the weather and knew the best techniques for farming. Often the priest consulted with Keeper of Stories in matters of medicine.

Each Cherokee village is made of two societies. The Red Society comprises the hunters and warriors. The White Society handles civil issues and commerce. Keeper of Stories was consulted by both the Red-and White Societies on a wide range of issues. Equally part of the clan is the Beloved Woman. She is well-respected and often consulted, her opinion warmly welcomed within the tribe.

As time passed, Traveling Wolf married a beautiful young woman from another clan. Together they had two sons in as many summers. Each time the young father went on a long hunt, or off to war, Keeper of Stories assured him that he'd look after his family, just as his friend had looked after him. Hearing these words brought up the guilt in his heart for avoiding him later in childhood. He looked into the eyes of his friend and said, "I've always trusted in your words, and I couldn't leave my family in better care than yours. You have truly become one of the most loved and cherished men of our tribe."

Keeper of Stories smiled. "Traveling far, and fighting to keep our nation and people safe, is a proud and noble thing; yet sometimes we have to learn to bloom where we are planted."

After Traveling Wolf had left with the rest of the warriors, Little Dove approached her son and asked, "Did you mention to your friend that you are ill?" "No, mother, I did not. My friend is going off to war, and I did not want to worry him."

Little Dove squeezed his hand. "Son, you're a good man and I am very proud of you."

"If I am good man, mother, then I am but a reflection of your good work," responded Keeper of Stories, squeezing her hand back.

Days later, he still had health issues, and was getting weaker. However, he kept on telling stories to calm the fears of the villagers with the men off to war.

Twenty-three days had passed since the warriors had left. The sons of Traveling Wolf were playing at the edge of the village when Climbing Bear, the eldest, was bitten on the leg by a rattlesnake, a venomous pit viper. The boy was taken home, and the Medicine Man came to do all in his power to save him; he thought the boy would surely die. Yet Keeper of Stories wasn't going to let that happen. He applied all his knowledge, sitting with the boy for many days; had cool spring water carried in to help keep his fever down, and drained what poison he could from the boy's leg, using a variety of herbs to treat the child. Keeper of Stories grew himself weaker but would not give up. One morning, the child looked up at him and said, "I'm hungry." The fever had come down, and the infection around the bite had begun to heal. The boy made a full recovery, only leaving a bad scar from dead tissue caused by the snake bite.

The news was not so good for his healer. By the time the warriors returned victorious, he had grown too weak to get up and move around. Traveling Wolf's wife, Passion Flower, ran into her husband's arms and told him what had happened; how Keeper of Stories had saved the life of their son Climbing Bear. She told him how ill his friend now was.

As he reached him, Little Dove and the Medicine Man were with him. He pressed the hand of his old friend. As he did so, he opened his eyes and in a weak voice whispered, "It's good that you are here. I feared I would not see you of this world again."

Traveling Wolf attempted a smile. "I'm right here with you. Thank you for being there for my family and saving the life of Climbing Bear."

"I did all I could, but it was the Creator who did most. We only serve in this world until He calls us back to the Sacred Mountain."

Even in his weak state, Keeper of Stories exchanged tales of their youth with his old friend, recounting their shared adventures.

"I do have a confession to make and beg your forgiveness," said the warrior by his friend's sickbed. "When I was first training to be a warrior, I sometimes went the long way out of the village because I felt guilty and ashamed that I did not spend more time with you. The thought of you sitting there, waiting in vain for me, has laid heavy in my heart for many years."

Keeper of Stories responded with the hint of a smile. "There is nothing to forgive. I always knew of-and felt your pain. We all have our own path to walk in this life. You were always my friend, and I was happy to be there for you should you need me, as you always were for me. Oh, the virtues of childhood, I wish we could hold them dearer as we grow older."

These were the last words of Keeper of Stories. He closed his eyes, and the last breath left his body. The wise man began his way to the Sacred Mountain. Great warrior that he was, Traveling Wolf wept like a child.

Later in the afternoon, he walked to the big rock that overlooked the river where the friends had come so many times before. As the sun was setting, he returned to the village. He passed a group of women, one of whom was saying, "My sister had poison ivy on both her arms, and he told her to use the watery sap of Jewelweed to stop the itching and dry it up." As he passed by other groups, it become clear that they were all talking of Keeper of Stories. During this time, it was common not to mention the name of the deceased until it was claimed by another person. A group of men were talking about the legend of the Cedar Tree, and a group of children discussed the tales of Arrow Woman and the Sacred Pipe. It seemed that everyone had tales to tell which Keeper of Stories had made popular.

Passion Flower was with the children and Little Dove, when he arrived home. She looked to her husband and said, "Do you notice how everyone is sharing his stories and teachings?"

He looked up to the stars. "Yes, I noticed the same as I was walking through the village. He will always be remembered, as will the stories he taught us all. He once told me, 'The Creator, the Master of the Universe, offers us opportunities to go beyond our limitations. And so it shall always be.'"

A Forever Home

Bob owned and operated a small long-haul trucking business. He'd been gone from home for two weeks, so he decided to service all his trucks, and take the week off to be with his family. On Sunday morning, just after breakfast, his phone rang. His friend and attorney Jim was on the other end of the line.

"If you're not working tomorrow, could you meet me at my office? I want you to come to Richmond with me to look at a 1972 Nova SS that's for sale. As you know, I've wanted one for a long time, but I want to make sure it's worth what the seller is asking for."

"Sure, I'll be at your office at 10:00 tomorrow morning."

The next day, Bob took his three-year-old daughter Ashley along to Jim's office. From there, they continued in Bob's car. Ashley's seat was already in it.

The Nova SS didn't look bad at first glance, but some of the bodywork was poorly done; Jim decided not to buy it.

On the way back, they traveled via a backroad, passing by a house with several old cars dotted around it, and a couple of junk piles. Ashley pulled a pained expression and said, "Look at that big dog, his chain is so short...it's chocking him."

Her father stopped the car.

Jim knocked on the door of the house to try and get the owner to help the dog, but no one was home. The big German Shepherd kept barking, trying to break free. The owner had placed a logging chain around its neck, securing it with a cheap padlock. It had twisted into so many knots that it was now only about two feet long; the other end was bolted to a steel rod and driven deep into the ground.

Bob let the dog smell the back of his hand, after which it let Bob pet it. The animal was standing in mud, without food or water. Jim said, "I got the address. I'll call this in."

"You might not have to," said Bob. Since he'd got out of prison in 1982, he was used to carrying a homemade tension bar and pick. He went to work on the cheap lock. Within a few minutes, he forced it open. He put his belt around the dog's neck with Jim's help. Finally, he removed the chain from the German Shepherd's neck. It revealed a sad sight. The dog displayed a raw ring around its neck from wearing a chain without collar. Jim led it over to the car; Bob meanwhile fetched a cup and poured some of Ashley's water into it so it could have a drink. He then moved Ashley's car seat up front. Walking around the car, he forcefully threw the padlock through the window of the house. It smashed through the glass with a bang.

"Damn, Bob, you're the only one I know who'll do something really good only to make a crime out of it at the last minute," huffed Jim.

"Well, with how the owner has been treating this dog, he's not going to say a word. You'll drive now, and I'll sit with the dog."

"Once we get back to my office, I'll call around for a vet. Let's have the dog checked out and see what can be done about the raw ring around its neck. With you throwing the lock through the guy's window, I won't be able to call the authorities."

Jim carried Ashley into his office, and Bob led the dog in. As soon as he'd shut the door, he relieved it of the belt around its neck. The dog immediately ran over to Jim's receptionist Lynda, standing close to her, all the while looking up at her out of big, sad eyes. Lynda gave it her lunch and fetched a bowl of water. Jim explained to her how the German Shepherd had come to be with them. She phoned the vet who told her to bring the animal straight in. She kept petting the dog, who lapped up the attention. "I'll take him to the vet, Jim. But I want to keep him. He's so adorable."

Jim glanced over at Bob. "What do you think?"

"I think the dog adopted Lynda at first sight and now seems to have found a happy forever home."

Lynda grabbed a long silk scarf from her bag. "This won't hurt his neck on the drive to the vet."

Jim walked him over to the door when Ashley ran to him. "I want to pet him some more…please!"

Jim offered to buy Ashley and Bob lunch across the street. On the way out, she asked her dad whether they could come to see the dog from time to time. She'd quickly grown fond of him. They had to find out what Lynda would name him, for starters.

"Sure we can. Lynda would like that a lot."

"Dad, can we also get ice cream, please?"

Bob smiled at Ashley. "Daughter, did you just try to con your dad?"

Ashley held up her thumb and mommy finger, indicating a small amount, and said, "Yep, buddy, just a little bit."

Ashley got ice cream before they got home. While licking it, all kinds of great names for the German Shepherd with the pretty eyes floated through her head.

She would make a list and show Lynda.

Work Ethic

On most days after school, nine-year-old Madison and ten-year-old Jimmy walked their mid-sized, white dog Roscoe along the railway tracks. Judging by his size, color, and curled tail, Roscoe likely had some Husky in him. The children carried a five-gallon metal bucket for the blocks of coal they picked up, which had fallen from passing trains; where the terrain allowed, they'd pull a small, homemade wagon along to hold two five-gallon buckets of coal.

If the coal supply at home was low, they added their pickings to it, but more often they sold the coal and saved the money. The children gathered and cut kindling and firewood to sell, too. A few elderly people paid them to help with their garden, and canning vegetables. The children went along the sides of the mountain to pick blackberries, once ripe, to sell. They always looked for opportunities to work and make money, saving every cent.

Jimmy and Madison were saving for three items in particular: one, a nice sweater for their grandmother; two, a mother's ring with her late husband's birthstone at the center, and those of her children on each side; third and not least, a headstone for their late father's grave with his picture on it. Each Sunday after church, the children went to the bedroom and counted the money they had made. Each time they went to town with their grandmother Lilly they made payments toward the items.

By the first week of December, they had paid for the mother's ring and for the sweater; with what little money the siblings had left, they paid for their father's headstone. As Jimmy was counting out the money to Mr. Noe, the shopkeeper, a middle-aged man walked through the door. Ransom Noe looked up at him. "Hello, Paul. I'll be with you in a few minutes."

Paul smiled. "Take your time. I'm in no hurry."

While her brother was counting out the money, Madison blurted out, full of excitement, "This is the mother's ring we got mom and the sweater for granny!"

Paul smiled at the girl's excitement when showing Ransom the Christmas gifts.

Jimmy said proudly, "We paid for those gifts. That's why we don't have more money this time. We'll have more next time."

Ransom put the children at ease. "That'll be just fine. If you'd like, I'll have Kathy take you to her office and help you with the wrapping."

An innocent smile beamed across Madison's face. "That would be really nice, Mr. Noe." Kathy turned to help Jimmy and Madison with their gifts. After they'd gone up to the office, Paul stepped up and said, "Those sure seem to be really sweet children."

Ransom nodded. "Paul, you don't know the half of it. They've been working relentlessly to save for these Christmas gifts. They've been making small payments toward a headstone for their father's grave. He was killed in action last year. The children heard their mother say how handsome he was in his uniform after he was drafted. They want to get him a headstone with a hinged brass fixture for his picture. They want everyone to see how handsome he was."

Paul said, "The Army should provide a headstone. It can take time, but I will look into it through the Veterans of Foreign Wars. What was their father's name?"

"James Carlos Napier. Don't forget, the children have their hearts set on a headstone with his picture on it."

"I remember the name. Some of our members helped with the funeral. He was awarded the Purple Heart and the Bronze Star. I'm sure there were other distinctions too. Ransom, do you believe it would be okay for me to talk to the children? Do you know how to get in touch with their mother?"

"I'm sure they would love that. As for their mother, her name is Lois and she works over at the A&P grocery. She lives with the children's grandmother over on Cranks Creek, on their old home place. James and Lois met because their fathers were best friends. They were both killed along with two other miners over at the Harlan Fuel Coal Mines at Yancey in 1959. They've had a rough go of it…but these are wonderful children."

Kathy, Jimmy, and Madison, returned to the lobby and showed off their wrapped gifts.

Ransom said, "You've done a great job, they look just beautiful. Now, this man here is Paul Short. He owns and operates the local auto-parts store. He is also the post commander at the VFW. Would it be okay if he talks with you?"

Jimmy nodded. Madison was still enamored with the pretty wrapping paper.

A choked-up Paul said, "If it's okay with you, I want to help you with your father's headstone. He was a hero. He gave his life for our country, and it would be an honor to help you."

Madison asked, "Will it have his picture on it?"

"Yes, if that's what you'd like. Just show Mr. Noe what you want, and I will get it ordered. The VFW will pay for it in honor of your father's service. We will also display a big picture of your father at the VFW with his name, rank, and awards listed," replied Paul.

"How long will it take?" asked Jimmy. The children were happy to have his unexpected help.

Mr. Short said that the picture would arrive in time for Christmas, and that Mr. Noe would tell everyone once the headstone was set in place, probably around early springtime.

"That's perfect," cheered Madison, "dad loved spring!"

At the A&P, Madison and Jimmy told their grandmother and mother about their talk with the men, about the headstone, and the picture that would be put up at the VFW. They kept the mother's ring and sweater a secret, however.

The following day, Paul stopped by the store and spoke with Lois Napier about three things: the headstone for their father, which he had now ordered; the portrait of James C. Napier going on permanent display in the main hall of the VFW; lastly, Paul invited Mrs. Napier and her family to the VFW Christmas party to be held on December 23rd.

Lois was a little overwhelmed with a sudden sensation of gratitude. "Mr. Short, I didn't know the children were doing any of this. I was sure they were working toward something…but I never dreamed of this. I've been putting in extra hours to get caught up on bills and to make sure the children have a nice Christmas."

"I understand. And if there is anything you need, we will always be here for you."

Lois smiled at such kindness. "It's been rough, truth be told. But we are adjusting…the children are resilient. Overall, we're doing okay. After church on Sunday, I'll be taking them up the mountain to cut a Christmas tree. Their father used to do it with them. It'll be something special."

"That's nice. It's good to adhere to traditions. And to create new ones, in time. Please remember, you and the children are part of our family at the VFW now."

The following Friday morning it began snowing. In a very short time, a white blanket covered the roads. School classes were cancelled for the rest of the day, so that the school buses could get the children home safely; Madison and Jimmy reached home by 11:00 a.m. Their grandmother Lilly had made cookies. She let the kids have some, even though they'd not eaten their school lunches yet. "Before the snow gets worse, I'm going to walk down to Mr. and Mrs. Jackson and bring them cookies. I'll be back in less than half an hour," she said.

When Lilly returned home, the children and Roscoe were gone. They had left a note on the kitchen table which read, 'We are going up the mountain to cut a Christmas tree. Mom will be so surprised! We'll be home before it gets dark'.

Lilly called Lois at the A&P and suggested she should come home straight away. She was about to start home when she learned that the road across Cranks Creek Mountain was closed due to the snow.

When calling the rescue squad and sheriff's department, she got the same reply: The road remained closed, and the children hadn't been missing long and would likely be home before a search could get underway. Lois then called Paul and explained the situation. "Do you have a jeep that can get over the mountain?"

Paul said he did, but that the police wouldn't let anyone up there until snowplows had cleared the road. "I have an idea, let me just make a call," he said. He talked with a young veteran who visited the post from time to time. He lived less than a mile from the Napier home. He called Lois back, informing her that his friend was already on the way to Lilly, to start a search for the children. "He was raised in the mountains. He spent two tours of duty in Vietnam as a sniper, both near and behind enemy lines. In other words…he knows what he's doing," he reassured the worried mother.

"What's his name?"

"Balinger Roughwater. He says he knows you and your family."

"Yes, when I was a freshman in high school, Bal was a senior. Thanks a lot, Paul."

"Do you have anywhere to stay until the mountain is cleared?"

"Yes," said Lois, "I have a cousin living here in town."

"Alright, as soon as the road is cleared I will put a search team together and we'll cross the mountain together."

Bal arrived at the Napier home with his black-and-white Paint Horse, Comanche, and his German Shepherd dog, Apollo. Lilly showed him the note the children had left. "They wore their boots and heavy winter clothing, and took their school lunches with them. Their dog Roscoe is with them. Oh, and a hatchet and flashlight are also missing."

Bal nodded. "Smart kids. May I bring my dog in and let him smell some of their things? There will be whiteout conditions higher on the mountain, and Apollo will be of great help. I know a few areas with nice evergreens which is what the children are looking for."

When Bal set out, he led Comanche and Bear to walk out in front of him. The trail the children had taken had several switchbacks, and many other trails ran off the main one. Visibility was very poor in the blowing snow; two hours into his search, Bal noticed a snow-covered hump in the middle of a trail fork. He picked up a freshly cut evergreen tree, shaking off the snow. Bal said to himself, 'These are smart kids. They took the wrong trail, but they marked their way with the tree.'

About forty minutes later, Apollo began barking. Another dog barked back. He found the children beneath a cliff overhang. They had made a small fire with dry wood, which someone had left under the cliff, as is common in mountain life.

Barely within earshot, Bal shouted, "My name is Balinger Roughwater, but you can call me Bal. Your grandmother Lilly sent me out to find you. I found your Christmas tree along the trail. Marking your way was very smart of you."

"The snow got so bad we didn't know which way to go. We remembered what dad used to say…in bad weather find shelter and make a fire if you can," said Jimmy.

"Your dad told you right, and you did just what you were supposed to do. Here, I have a small tent and large sleeping bag to share. I brought a small heater, too. You won't have to freeze as much. I'll prepare warm food and hot chocolate. There's food for the dogs and horse too, in the saddle bags."

Bal hoped the children would eat, get warm and go to sleep, but they preferred to lie in the tent with the front flap open so they could talk. They spoke about their dad, how he'd been killed in the war. They told him about the headstone, and how they were making money to save up for it.

Madison hit Bal with a big question. "Were you in the war with our father?"

"Yes, I was there."

"I'm glad you didn't die like daddy did," said Madison.

On hearing this innocent, heartfelt sentence, Bal choked up. He was lost for words.

"Were you afraid in the war?" asked Jimmy.

"Oh yes," said Bal, "sometimes a little…sometimes a lot. It's a bit like how you felt today. You got lost in the snow, and I'm sure you were afraid. Yet you did what you had to to look out for each other. That's exactly what soldiers do. They take care of each other, especially when they're afraid."

They talked well into the night. The dogs curled up next to the siblings in the tent. Bal realized that this was the first time he had opened up about his service since he'd left the Army. Just when he thought that the kids had gone to sleep, Jimmy whispered, "Bal, will you come to Christmas dinner with us?"

"Well, your mom and grandmother will have to agree to that."

"I'm sure they will say yes," said Jimmy, smiling in the dark.

"Please bring Apollo, too," said Madison.

Bal kept a small fire going throughout the night; as morning approached, the snow slowed and some visibility returned, but several inches still covered the ground. He put water by the fire to heat up an oatmeal breakfast for the children. He fed Comanche and packed things up, while the kids got up. After breakfast, he placed Jimmy and Madison on Comanche, wrapping the sleeping bag around them to keep them warm on the way down. When they reached the fork in the trail, he tied a line to the tree on the ground so that the horse could drag it along.

By 9:15 a.m., Lois, Paul, and several men from the VFW, had crossed the mountain and arrived at the Napier home. It was still snowing when the men got their gear together. Soon they heard dogs approaching, their barking growing louder. They cheered when through the haze and snow, they glimpsed the image of a man leading a horse. Two children were riding it. Paul yelled for Lois to come outside. Bal lifted Madison and Jimmy off Comanche. "Are you two okay…are you hurt…hungry?" worried the mother.

"We are alright, mom," said Madison. The children didn't look as if they'd been through an ordeal; on the contrary, they seemed happy and smiley. "We slept in a tent under a big cliff, and we had oatmeal for breakfast. It tasted yummy. And guess what, Bal was in the Army too, just like daddy." Jimmy said, "We asked him to come for Christmas dinner. That's okay, isn't it, mom?"

"Bal went and found you and brought you home. Of course he has an open invitation to dinner."

Paul quietly said to his men, "Look at the glow on Bal's face. He's been in a dark place since returning from the war. These children have rescued him as much as he rescued them. A great blessing for Bal, with all he's been through."

Lois brought out a large pot of coffee and offered a cup to her children's saviour. But Bal declined. He had to tend to his livestock.

"Wait a second," said Paul, "old JT is at your place tending to your stock. He was keen to help out in his own way, given that he's too old to climb a snow-covered mountain."

Bal stayed for a cup of hot coffee. He agreed to come over for Christmas dinner. Paul said, "As you know, our Christmas party at the post is on December 23rd. I'll get Lois and her family set at the table with you." Bal couldn't help but grin in a childlike way.

Paul smiled at the veterans. "This feeling right here is what it's all about. Now let's get a base made for the Christmas tree so the children can have fun decorating it. It's a magical time of year."

My Best Friend

In the early 1900s, a young German-Irish couple emigrated to the United States. After settling in the state of Pennsylvania, Uwe and Ilona Brennan made their way to Harlan County, Kentucky. At the very head of Catron Creek, Uwe went to work in the coal mines for the Golden Glow Coal Company.

The couple never had any children, but they were well-respected and loved in the community. The Great Depression officially started in 1929. Jobs were difficult to find, even more so to hold down. The Golden Glow Coal Company stayed in business, but wages were low. Uwe had become a section foreman at the mines. Without children, the pair was able to save a little, even in these difficult times; their dream was to buy a small farm in the green hills of Harlan County. Often, when a miner got injured or fell sick, Uwe took on the shift so the miner would have no loss of wages. Ilona helped as a midwife and tended to children in the community when a mother fell ill. Their most prized possession was a black-and-white Border Collie they named Ring due to the white ring of hair around his neck. When Uwe wasn't working, Ring was right by his side. During the day, while he was down the mines, Ring followed Ilona's every step.

In this era, when an accident, roof fall, or explosion, occurred at the mine, there was no rescue team to call in to help. If something happened, a very loud steam whistle was sounded; this alerted the other shift of miners, who'd swiftly stand in as a rescue team.

By the later part of the 1930s, the economy was improving. Many of the mines were now unionized, while some fights over unionization continued.

Uwe and Ilona were close to having enough money to purchase the farm they so wanted. He was close to retirement. After a lifetime of work, he was looking forward to the serenity of farm life. One summer morning upon reaching work, Uwe noticed that the midnight shift had not shored up the ceiling with the timbers required. He pulled his workers back to safety, then went to work with the timber setters.

Ilona had done the laundry and was now outside, hanging her wash onto the clothesline to dry. Ring was by her side when the steam whistle was sounded, calling in the next shift of miners to help. A neighbor who was feeding her chickens also looked toward the mine at the sound of the whistle; seconds later, she witnessed Ilona fall to the ground. She yelled for help and ran to where her neighbor had collapsed; yet when help arrived, Ilona was already dead.

By the end of the day, it was understood that there'd been a roof collapse, and only one miner had been killed - that miner had been Uwe. It was as if Ilona intuitively knew that her husband had been killed at hearing the baleful whistle sound.

The couple was buried side-by-side next to the church on the southern side of the coal camp, after one of the largest turnouts for a funeral in Harlan County. Uwe and Ilona had made arrangements in case of their deaths. Their savings and belongings were to be donated to the church. The only other provision in their will stated that Arlis Pennington was to have their dog, Ring. At this time, Arlis was a twelve-year-old boy, the son of the neighbor who'd seen Ilona fall to the ground. Ring loved running over to play with him, and it was obvious that he loved the dog.

Ring followed Arlis everywhere he went except to school. He waited excitedly when he got back home. Over time, the dog taught the boy much about loyalty, courage, devotion and respect. Ring slept next to his bed each night. The two became inseparable.

Arlis, and many others in the community, took notice of how Ring trotted past the graveyard where Uwe and Ilona lay buried. He ran over and sat between their graves, barking a few times. Coming or going, Ring always kept to this ritual, as if stopping to say hello.

Arlis joined the Army and fought in the last two years of World War Two. When he returned, his loyal, barking companion had gotten older but was pleased to be back with his master; for several more years, the dog did not leave his side. Up until his death, Ring always stopped at the graveyard.

Arlis lived up into his 80s. He often paid a visit to say hello to his deceased friends, just as his loyal dog had always done. Not long before Arlis died, he told his grandson about Ring and how the animal came to be with him.

After learning of the story, and up until this very day, his grandson regularly stops by the graveyard to say hello to his grandfather, and to Uwe and Ilona. He saves a special hello for Ring for being his grandfather's loyal friend.

Hayley

The park ranger truck was moving agonizingly slow while making its way up the narrow two-way mountain road. The driver, Ned Barker, looked over to Park Ranger Hayley Shell and asked, "Are you sure about this? We'll be at the trail in twenty minutes, and it will be an hour at least until first light."

"Yes, I'm sure," replied Hayley. Someone is trapping and taking live bears…not to mention the ones they kill and butcher on site. We have to put a stop to it."

Ned said, "I understand it's our job. My point is, you'll be out there on your own in the dark with the poachers and the bears and other creatures that injure and kill."

"Thanks for your concern, but I'll be fine. Keep your radio on. If I need backup, I'll call you. Otherwise pick me up at noon."

Sleepy-eyed Ned said, "Well, alright then. Oh, by the way, Tina and I saw your music video last night. It's come out really nice."

"Thanks. Beth had the idea to make a more modern version of *Traveling Man*, so I changed the perspective and made it *Traveling Girl*. A beautiful woman in country dress came out for some of the shots."

"Did Beth get jealous?"

"Nah, there was no time…she was right there with me."

"Well, maybe you'll get rich and famous, and I'll be able to tell people I worked with you when you were a ranger."

Hayley laughed. "Not sure about the famous part. Some money would be nice, though. I could do more with the help of my brother and his family. But I like my job…for now. I'm only testing the waters in the music business."

When they reached the trail, Hayley grabbed her pack; besides her sidearm, she took with her a 12-gauge pump action shotgun. A gentle breeze whispered through the dim, starlit night. She gave her eyes a moment to adjust, then faded into the darkness like a ghost. She knew the trail well. She'd worked it several times before and knew each and every path leading off it. She moved along quietly.

A grey shroud lit the sky at dawn. She reached the first fork in the trail and studied the surroundings for any sign of someone recently passing. No luck.

The second path yielded no sign either, yet between the second and third a large stone caught her eye. It was pressed down into the soft soil and carried a scuff mark on top. As she searched the edge of the trail, she located foliage pressed into the soil; gently placing her fingers under it to lift it, she exposed a large boot print. She determined that four to six men had passed through several hours ago, and it appeared that they were carrying something heavy.

Hayley knew it was too late to overtake the group, but her nagging mind wondered why they'd turned into the valley in the first place. There wasn't a road or trail, merely a stream about fifty feet wide and roughly knee-to-waist deep. It was too shallow to get a boat up on it. To reach a boat or trail, the poachers would have had to climb up the nearest ridge with a heavy load, which didn't make sense.

She decided to backtrack and find out where else they'd been. As she walked on, she located a place where something off the high bank had been slid onto the trail. Someone had attempted to cover it, but that was done poorly in a haste, perhaps because the person believed that someone was coming this way.

Hayley had grown up in Western North Carolina, tracking and hunting with her father and grandfather. She had spent eight years in the Marine Corps and was well-trained for the job she was undertaking. A few hundred feet up the mountain, the poachers had all but stopped trying to cover their tracks. Hastening her steps, while keeping sight of the marks the culprits had left, she worked her way up the mountain until she reached a cove with thick laurel growth. Right here, she located a homemade live trap with the remains of a slaughtered bear. The tracks informed her that the live bear was likely a cub and the remains probably a sow. The hide, meat, and some organs, were missing from the grotesque scene. Hayley collected DNA samples of the remains. She also located a .308 spent rifle cartridge, a crumpled-up cigarette pack, and a few cigarette butts. She collected all items in evidence bags to aid in her investigation. Finally, she marked the location on her GPS.

She stood erect, overlooking the mountains and valley below, enjoying the tranquillity the scenery offered; this morning, however, the bestial torture and slaughter of a bear, and her cub likely being carried off, diminished any remnants of serenity. She surmised that the cub had been captured, and that the sow was killed while trying to free it. The poachers appeared to have been in a rush, which was unlike other scenes the rangers had located, again indicating they suspected that someone was coming.

The live trap had not been reset, so Hayley decided not to destroy it. She cleared away her tracks, leaving no sign that she had located it; in fact, she left not a single footprint, scuffed stone, or broken twig on site. Once she returned onto the main trail, she made it appear as if she'd passed right by. She continued until four further paths branched off it. At that point, she returned the way she'd come, making sure not to leave any clear sign of her passing.

Before she reached the point on the main road where Ned was supposed to pick her up, an eerie feeling caused her to shudder. The culprits had known she was coming, and only two people in the world knew of her plan – her supervisor Billy Nolan, and Ned. The latter was waiting in the car, and now casually asked, "Locate anyone or anything?"

She shook her head, not giving away her suspicions. "Not a thing. Turned into quite a nice morning hike."

"Well, you cannot find what isn't there. We might get lucky next time."

Hayley shot her partner a stealthy look of contempt. She said nothing else until they got back to the ranger station.

Ned continued on his rounds alone. Hayley went to see Bill Nolan. She had known him for a very long time and knew he'd never have any part in poaching activity. She confessed her suspicion; apart from Bill, only Ned knew she'd be on the trail this morning, and she was sure they'd known of her coming. She turned over the evidence and suggested he keep it to himself until they figured it all out. Bill agreed, then reminded her of the talk she was to give at the high school the next day. It was her weekend off. "Any plans?"

"Well, on Saturday, Beth and I will just hang out, maybe catch a movie, then dinner somewhere. On Sunday, we'll be spending the day with my brother Tony and his family."

"That will do you good. It will give both of us a little time to figure out what to do about these poachers."

Early Friday morning, dressed in her park ranger uniform, Hayley gave a speech to freshman-and sophomore students. She explained the important job of a park ranger, and how it covered many diverse aspects, from the safety of visitors to the care for the forest and wildlife. After her talk, she took questions.

One student said, "We googled you. The park service appears to have a lot of great career opportunities. We also saw that you were a Marine and were awarded the Purple Heart. Wow. Can you tell us about the Marines and what it meant when you were awarded the medal?"

"One can make a good career out of any branch of the military," said Hayley. "I joined the Marines to make a career out of it, and to further my education. I served on two tours of Iraq, and as you probably discovered, was wounded on the second. The Humvee I was in with three other Marines was struck by an IED. Two of us stayed conscious and got the other two out of the wreckage. We treated their wounds – and ours – as best as we could, keeping the enemy at bay until help arrived."

"Did everyone survive? And how did you even function in a situation like that? Weren't you paralyzed by fear?"

"All four of us lived, but one lost an arm and a leg. As for being afraid, yes, I was terrified. The dilemma could neither be surmounted nor escaped. The desperate nervous tension drained my strength, but strangely replenished it at the same time. Difficult to explain. Then after eight years with the Marines, I retired to join the U.S. Park Service."

The student had clearly carried out detailed research into her history on Google. He was moving on to the obvious, more light-hearted topic. "We watched your music video. It was great. And…you looked really hot in it." Students at the back of the class giggled. "You have a pretty girlfriend, an attorney, right? Did you date boys or girls in high school? Or both? Isn't that a bit greedy?"

Hayley laughed. She enjoyed this refreshingly open line of questioning. These young students were excited by a dose of real-world experience. "I dated both, but probably not out of greed. Later in life I found that I was most attracted to strong, intelligent, attractive women."

The same student kept the questions firing. "How old were you when you came out?"

"I never came out, technically. I've never felt the need to put a label on myself like a product on a grocery store shelf. I knew who I was, and that mattered. I have always followed my heart and tried to make decisions that fit my personality."

"Anyone at the park service ever give you a hard time over having a girlfriend?"

Another student took the reins, pre-empting Hayley's answer. "Of course not, she's a Marine and who'd want to mess with a Marine? She'd kick their butts!" Loud laughter filled the classroom. The teacher stepped in, as if to break up a minor riot. "Mind your manners, students, mind your manners."

Hayley kept her cool. "Again, let me stress how important it is to get a good education and to try and make a career of something you really want to do in life. Build your skills, then put them to good use. Well, that's enough from me."

On Sunday, Hayley and Beth visited her brother Tony. After cooking steaks on the grill, they sat on the back porch with Tony and his wife Karen. Their boys came running up, asking Hayley to come to the creek with her. They were keen to show her something they were building for the Boy Scouts.

Hayley walked with the boys, Junior and Mike. They were excited about the small raft they'd been working on. "Dad is going to help us float it down to grandpa's house," Junior said. At that moment, it hit Hayley: The poachers couldn't get a boat up the stream, but they could fit a raft onto it!

On Monday morning, she met with Bill and told him that her young nephews might have helped her crack the case. The two began searching through the roads and trails leading over into the valley from the far side of the ridge, on the station computer. The absence of any noticeable road or trail baffled them.

Later that morning, Hayley drove to the far side of the ridge, traveling up to the very last house. She stepped out of the car. No one appeared to be around. She then heard a woman faintly crooning a lullaby from a screened-in back porch. She approached her quietly. She was careful not to startle the woman as she was putting her baby down for a nap. In a soft voice she said, "Hi. My name is Hayley Shell, and I'm with the Park Service. Is it okay to come on the porch and talk with you?"

"Sure, come up and have a seat," said the young mom. "I'm Clara. I know you. My husband Frank used to work with your brother Tony."

Hayley commented on a beautiful Cherokee Rose bush growing by the steps of the porch. Clara smiled. "It was a gift from my grandmother. She loved the old legends of our people. The Cherokee Rose is a reminder of how our ancestors were treated and forced to leave their homelands under the Removal Act. I've also heard that the spirit of the Cherokee Rose grows in the hearts, symbolizing courage and hope."

"Your grandmother sounds like a very special lady. Now, I need to talk to you about a different matter. Do you happen to know of a road or trail that leads over to the stream in the valley behind the ridge?"

"Yes, I do," replied Clara, "there is one. You can go on up in about three quarters of a mile. It is an old game trail leading to the stream. It never used to be much of a path until people in 4-wheelers made it noticeable. At this time of year, it turns into a tunnel of trees."

"Could you get a 4-wheel-drive pickup to the stream that way?"

Clara thought about it for a moment. "I guess you could get within a hundred feet of it. I sometimes go that way with my husband."

Hayley asked whether she had noticed anything odd about the people coming and going. Clara said that a few times two pickup trucks had come by with several men, carrying rubber rafts on each, even though the stream wasn't wild enough for rafting. One of the trucks was driven by a man, the other by a woman. They must have headed down to the stream, said Clara.

"Did you know who they were? Can you describe the trucks?"

"They were both old-model Fords, one blue, one red. I didn't know the man, but I did know the woman. It was Tina Hill. I went to school with her. She was two years ahead of me, but I remember her well."

Hayley took notes. Before leaving she said, "Your beautiful boy seems to be ready for his nap. I'll leave my card here on the table for you. If you see the trucks return, please give me a call. Thank you for being so helpful."

Hayley drove back to the ranger station. She told Bill Nolan what Clara had told her. She mentioned the name Tina Hill.

"That could be the same Tina Hill Ned has been dating. What do you think?" asked Bill.

"I'm not sure, but I will get a photo and drive out again to confirm either way."

Bill suggested that she'd do that later. He was quite sure that this was the same Tina Hill who Ned was seeing. "I've been digging into Ned," he said, "looking into his family, and Tina and her family. Ned and his family live clean lives. However, Tina Hill's family is a different matter. Her uncle and a few of her cousins have been convicted of poaching in the past. Other family members have committed robberies and drug-related crimes. I know how our Ned is head over heels in love with her. It could be that he is involved, or merely giving away too much information with pillow talk. Let's pull up that stream on the computer. Here…take a look. It passes under the highway, going up the mountain right here." He held a thumb onto the screen to mark the spot, and it almost eclipsed the entire view. He removed it. "I will put a hidden camera below the bridge. Let's hope we can catch the poachers passing downstream that way."

On the monitor, the two colleagues followed the flow of the stream into the river. It ran right behind Tina Hill's farm. Hayley said, "It all adds up now. But we are missing hard evidence."

Bill suggested to get a few pictures from the high school yearbook to confirm the identity of Tina Hill with Clara. He told Hayley that the team had located pans with a mixture of honey and whiskey, used as bear bait. These were currently being checked for prints.

Ten days passed until Hayley received a call from Clara, telling her about the same old-model Ford trucks passing by her house, rafts strapped to the roofs. Hayley called Bill, who put together a task force of rangers. Bill called Ned to his office and confronted him with the evidence. He denied having anything to do with the poaching but admitted talking too freely with Tina about park business. The look of stupidity on his face as he realised his blunders told Hayley and Bill that he was telling the truth.

Bill ordered Ned to hand in his pistol, badge, and phone, to the ranger at the desk. He was not to have any contact with anyone until the operation was over. "We'll talk then, and I really do hope you are telling the truth."

He said to Hayley, "I'm going to lead team one to the spot where the stream runs into the river. You'll take team two. Once we've made our arrest, your team will execute the warrant on the farm."

Hayley and four rangers, two per vehicle, were parked out of view of the house. She sent two others up the riverbank on foot from the south side. She slowly moved in along the riverbank from the north side with another ranger. The ground was soggy, wet as a sponge. She made her way to the edge of the tree line with the others, steadily, in calm fashion, staying out of sight until the very moment Bill would give the signal to move in. Hayley took note of a rowboat that was tied to a tree.

Just after sunrise, a car came speeding down the driveway; it came to a halt beside the farmhouse. Tina Hill got out and rushed in. Moments later, Bill Nolan's voice came in over the radio, "We have five suspects in custody, and we recovered one live bear cub. You are clear to execute your arrest warrant."

As the four rangers in vehicles approached the farmhouse, the backdoor flung open, and Tina Hill ran out toward the rowboat.

Hayley sprinted in a bid to overtake her. Tina grabbed a boat paddle and swung for her. Hayley ducked under the paddle and tackled Tina, knocking the breath out of her. She rolled her over and handcuffed her. Tina began screaming, "I knew something was wrong the moment Ned didn't come home!"

Hayley told Bill over the radio that one male and two female suspects were in custody. "We also located four bear cubs in cages, several bear hides, and two large freezers stuffed with bear meat and organs."

Tina tried to influence Hayley, but she cut her off. "I've always thought you were a nudnik, and you've proven me right."

By the end of the day, the poaching case made national news. Hayley called Beth. She was glad that the events of the day had drawn to a successful conclusion. Together with her beautiful lover, she went over to Tony's house. She told her nephews how showing her the raft, had helped her solve the case.

"What will they do with Ned?" asked Junior.

"He will likely get suspended for thirty days or more, then placed on probation for a long while. Ned is only guilty of putting too much trust in his girlfriend. And we've all done that once in a while," she added, grinning at Beth.

"Well, I guess that's not too bad for him," said the boy, who felt that Ned's punishment was mild, given how these animals had suffered.

Aunt Hayley explained it further. "I want you boys to remember that kindness is the oil which takes the friction out of life. Those of us who seem to deserve kindness least, need it the most. A reputation can be made in a moment. Character, however, is built over a lifetime. I've always believed that our true character is revealed by what we do when no one is around."

Together, the nephews quoted a sentence their dad enjoyed using: "There is no danger of getting eye strain from looking on the brighter side of life."

Hayley was glad that the boys were still willing to see the bright in Ned Barker.

Shade

Shade Spencer was born and raised in a poor area of the Appalachian Mountains. His mother, Vicky, died in childbirth; his grandfather, Jack, was killed in a logging accident. Shade was raised by his father Shelby and grandmother Kate. Shelby never held a regular job. He was what is known as a country wheeler-dealer. A hustler. He bought and sold anything he could turn a profit on. He liked to gamble at poker and was a very cunning cheat. He hauled whiskey for local bootleggers and left no stone unturned to make money. Shelby did not rob or steal in the general sense; instead, he conned people any way he could conceive of. He ingrained his way of life into his son at an early age.

Not even out of elementary school, Shade followed in his father's footsteps. In the 1960s, parents prepared healthy lunches for their children to take to school. He smelled an opportunity to sell the unhealthy variety - snack cakes, chips, and candy. Sometimes, he traded these items for the homemade lunches of other children. He traded or sold marbles, a popular playground game. He drilled a hole in a penny or nickel and put it on a string, selling his makeshift necklaces for fifty cents or a dollar.

When the boy was eleven years old, his father was caught cheating in a poker game. He was shot and killed. However, this did not change Shade's inherited ways. He kept on living as he was taught. Later, he was drafted into the Marine Corps and served a tour of duty in Vietnam; he spent the rest of his time in the Marines excelling at pistol shooting.

After leaving the service, Shade returned home and went back to hustling. To boost his income, he participated in shooting competitions, moving from one match to another, mostly victoriously. He was a decent poker player and did not need to cheat to win.

He thought that he had his life going just the way he wanted it until the woman he'd been seeing got pregnant. After receiving this news, Shade decided to change, and to become a much better father than his had ever been to him. He found a job with a towing service and made plans to ask his girlfriend to marry him. He shared them with his grandmother, who was very pleased to see her grandson mending his ways.

A few days later, Shade stopped by the garage of Don Fee, to collect payment for a tow he'd done for Don a day earlier. On Friday nights, Don had a poker game going in the back room of his garage. The game was just breaking up, in the early hours of Saturday morning, when Shade arrived. Don greeted him in a leisurely, relaxed manner. "Good to see you, my friend. Here's your money for the tow."

Tom, one of the players, said, "Should have charged him double. Don's the big winner from last night."

Shade replied, "No, just what he owes is fine. You all have a good day now."

As he walked out, Tom hissed after him in a teasing tone, "Whoever would have thought that Shade Spencer does not want the extra money?"

Later that afternoon, Deputy J.C. Miller arrested Shade while he was getting ready to tow a car. Miller said, "Shade Spencer, you are under arrest for the murder of Don Fee this morning, and for robbery of his garage." The deputy read him his rights and took him to jail.

At trial, Tom and the two other poker players testified that Shade left the garage before they did. The pistol used to kill Don was never located. Yet Deputy Miller made a deal with William Hensley, a witness, to drop a pending drug case against him; the latter just had to testify that he saw Shade return to the garage a second time on the morning Don Fee was killed. Given Shade's shady reputation, he was convicted and sent to prison.

His daughter was born shortly after he was sent down. He not once got to see her. Once in prison, he went back to his old ways, which were a perfect fit for prison life. His daughter was named Shayla. When she was four years old, his grandmother sent him pictures of her for the first time, as well as letters telling him what she was like. Then his grandmother passed away, and for the next six years, he heard no more about Shayla.

For ten years, Shade maintained that he was innocent.

He began to attend prison church. He prayed to God, promising that if he ever got out, he'd not do any further wrong, yet would instead dedicate his time to making life better for his daughter.

After ten years of wrongful imprisonment, Shade learnt that a man named Bill King robbed and killed a bank employee. The ballistics test on the pistol he'd used was a match to the one which killed Don Fee. Bill King was the first owner of the pistol, which was registered to him. He later admitted to robbing and killing Don. A few months later, Shade was set free.

Once outside, he moved into his grandmother's old, run-down home and began making repairs. He got a job as guide for tourists visiting the mountain hiking trail. He finally got to see Shayla regularly, on every other Sunday. He worked hard and saved as much money as he could to put toward his daughter having a good life and receiving a good education. He bought a lottery ticket each week and always played the same numbers, in the hope of hitting a nice payout to give to her.

One beautiful summer morning, Shade left on the trail with seven tourists – an elderly couple, a mother and her twelve-year-old son, a single, middle-aged woman, and an older man who seemed to be watched out for by a younger man.

He planned to take the group up the high trail, then down a switchback to the lower one, to return to the starting point. The overall hike would last around six hours. Shade didn't carry a weapon, only a daypack and a two-way radio, which was of little use except on the high points on the south side of the mountain.

He pointed out different trees and plants, and the tourists snapped pictures and seemed to be enjoying themselves.

The older man walked up front with the middle-aged man. Shade named distant mountain features. There was a low ridge to the left of the trail; on the right, a low drop-off of about four feet, and outcroppings of rock; below these, a rolling slope with a well-used game trail going downwards across the main trail.

Right then, several shots rang out. Shade saw the older man fall, and the younger one pulling him off to the edge for cover. He instructed the others to get behind the low bank of rocks. As he helped pull the older man to better cover, he noticed that the younger one had also been shot. The younger man turned and emptied his semi-automatic pistol toward the ridge where the shots were coming from, thus giving Shade more time to pull the old man to cover. As he fired, the younger one was struck again, and collapsed down to his hands and knees; he scrambled to make cover before passing out. Shade removed the first-aid kit from his daypack.

The older lady crawled over and said she was a retired nurse. "Let me see what I can do for them." Shade handed over the first-aid kit, then checked on everyone else. He tried to call for help on his two-way radio, yet to no avail. The retired nurse said, "This man is Federal District Judge Layton. He's been shot through his hip joint. He won't be able to walk, but he's not in immediate danger to his life. His Bailiff, Mr. Stewart, has two wounds to his mid-section. He does need medical attention right away." At this point, her husband stuck his head up and several shots were fired his way. The bullets came very close.

 Shade said, "I can't get anyone on the radio here. I need to be on top of the ridge or over the south side of the mountain, to get a signal. Those guys picked a good spot for an ambush. If we try to go either direction, they will have clear shots at us. There is the game trail, but it's at least forty yards before fading into the cover of trees."

Shade made his way over to where Mr. Stewart had dropped his pistol before collapsing. He'd dropped a Colt 1911 semi-automatic

.45 ACP, the same type Shade had used on the pistol team in the Marine Corps. It was empty.

Judge Layton pointed out that his bailiff kept two extra magazines in his jacket pocket.

Shade retrieved the two magazines and mumbled to himself that it wasn't much, but surely better than nothing. Then he talked to the child in the group. He had an idea.

He told the boy that he watched him run around the mountain like a deer. "Do you see the game trail running off to the right? It comes out above the big rock, where you were taking pictures earlier. If I can keep the shooters on the ridge busy, can you manage to run down to the big rock and use my two-way radio to get help?"

"Yes Sir, I can do that," said the boy, almost without hesitation. His mother objected instantly, saying that the plan was too dangerous. Shade knew she was right.

"Your name is Judy, right? Judy, it is dangerous, however, if we don't do something then none of us will get off this mountain alive."

Judy listened, and Shade continued detailing his plan. "Those two men can't move on their own, and we need to get help fast. There are at least two or three men up there firing on us. If only one of them proceeds to the high point on the trail, we'll have no cover, and we'll all die. My plan is this: Mr. Jones sticks his head up briefly and gets their attention. At that point I want Matt here to start running, while I advance out into the open, moving toward the assailants and firing. They will have no choice but to direct their fire at me. Matt is small and quick. He's our best hope. Our only hope, frankly."

He next explained his plan to the judge and the others in the group. "Once Matt is out of sight and the shooting has stopped, Judy will go first, Donna next, followed by Mr. and Mrs Jones. You all need to stay spread out until you reach the cover of trees. Keep on moving, right until you hit the main trail. Go as fast as you can."

Mrs. Jones said, "My husband and I will stay here. I need to help these men. If you fall, my husband will protect us any way he can with the judge's revolver."

Shade nodded. Yet there was still more he needed to tell the boy. Matt said that he'd talked the plan over with mum and that she was now on board with it.

"Boy, listen to me carefully. I've been a bullshit artist all my life. I spent ten years in prison for a crime I didn't commit. I always thought it was karma, due to my past. But I am being completely honest with you about this."

"I know you are, Mr. Spencer. I will do just as you tell me."

"If you do this, plainly speaking, I will be taking your childhood from you. You'll miss out on a lot. Once you take that first step, there is no turning back. From that point on you will think, act, and carry yourself like a man. At times you will feel good about it, and there will be times you'll realize how much you've missed. You won't fit in with others your age. Boy, are you sure you want to grow up this fast?"

"The thought of running out there and people shooting at me is crazy. But I know I can do it. I've made up my mind," insisted Matt.

"I know you're going to be a strong and honorable man. I'm going to try and survive this, but if I don't then I want you to look in on my daughter from time to time. I am blessed with a wonderful child, but, you know...I never really got to know her. Here, take my wallet. See, there is a picture with her contact information. Oh, and here's the lottery ticket. I buy one every week."

The boy took the wallet from Shade, briefly feeling the weight of responsibility like an unfamiliar shudder.

"Let me tell you something I was told when I first got to Vietnam. If you get shot, it will burn like fire, but you have to keep on moving, you do what you can to seek cover. If you go down, you're an easy target. Remember to keep on going, no matter what."

"You can count on me, Mr. Spencer. I want everyone to be safe."

"Alright, Matt, now go down to that last rock. Once Mr. Jones pops his head up, they will likely shoot to let us know they're watching. That's your cue. Sprint down that game trail toward the trees, and keep firm hold of the radio. I'll move into the open and return the fire. Even if I get hit, you still have at least fifteen to twenty seconds to get to those trees. Nothing to it."

Matt walked over to the rock. Mr. Jones, as per the plan, popped his head up. Just as he lowered it, two shots rang out. Matt started running like the wind as Shade stepped out into the open, returning fire. His advance took the two shooters on the ridge off guard, and they redirected their fire at him; they seemed to not notice Matt, who in a flash disappeared into the safety of the trees. Shade fired off two quick shots. Amid the counterfire, he took his time firing a third one. He was limited on bullets and wasn't using a long-range weapon. He took a round to the body and tumbled back. The shooting stopped. From instinct and Marine training, he discarded the empty magazine and put the loaded one in, not once taking his eyes off the ridge.

A few minutes passed without shots being fired.

"Mr. Spencer, I think you got them, or they ran away. Let me help you get back over here," said Mr. Jones.

"No, stay where you are," said Shade in a rasping voice, "I hit them, but I don't know how hard. I cannot feel my legs. I'd be of no use if you moved me. Did Matt and the women make it to the trees?"

Judge Layton confirmed that they did, and that his plan worked well.

"Good," sighed Shade, "Matt will fetch help."

Mrs. Jones whispered to the judge that Shade was badly hurt, but that they must keep talking and fighting to stay alive.

Judge Layton loudly asked, "How is it that you don't know your daughter?"

"Well, I was in prison for ten years for a crime I didn't commit."

"What was the charge?"

"Robbery and murder…but I used to tell myself that it was karma for all the bad I did in my past. In a way, it seemed fitting that I went to prison over something I didn't do. After my grandmother died, I got involved in the prison church. I made a deal with God to never do any further wrong if I made it out alive. Eventually they apprehended the man who committed the crime. I also learnt Deputy J.C. Miller had been asking my girlfriend out, only to be turned down. When he found out she was pregnant with my child, he used one of his drug dealers to have me sent to prison."

The judge said he'd read Shade Spencer's case in recent pleadings. He said that Deputy Miller was set for trial in his court in a week's time for federal drug-and racketeering charges.

"Looks like Deputy Miller is trying to get a new judge, maybe get two birds killed with one stone as a bonus," remarked Shade, sounding weaker. "I've just gone back on my promise to God and shot those two men. All I wanted was to live a good life, get my daughter a good education. I want her to have a life worth living and not be too ashamed of me."

"Mr. Spencer, when we get off this mountain, I will personally make sure that your daughter gets a good education. And Mr. Spencer…all of us have regrets in our past, and we try to make the best of what today has to offer. With what you have done today, your daughter will never be ashamed of you. I will make sure of that too. As for God. He knows you did what you had to do today. Mr. Spencer…*Shade*…can you hear me?"

In a gasping voice, Shade replied, "Yes, judge, I heard you. I feel full of smiles and butterflies and farting rainbows. Just trying to catch my breath."

Matt had reached the big rock, and after a few attempts, got someone on the two-way radio and explained the situation. The boy was still out of breath, yet when he mentioned that Federal Judge Layton and his bailiff were seriously injured, the man's voice on the other end took on a serious, urgent tone. "I'm Ranger Ellison and I will get help to you right away. Some campers in the valley already called in about hearing gunshots on the mountain. Ranger Carter is on his way up the trail. He has a two-way radio in his truck and is now heading your way. Go toward him and hurry him up until I can get more help sent."

Donna and Matt's mother arrived, and he told them that help was on its way. At that time, Ranger Carter appeared on the trail. Matt hurried toward him and filled him in on what had happened. Judy asked her son to go down the trail with her.

"No, mom, I'm going with Ranger Carter. You take the others back."

Mr. Jones handed the .38 pistol back to the judge. "I'll get the pistol from Mr. Spencer. I cannot hear him breathe anymore." He grabbed the weapon from Shade's hand and ran up the ridge. A few minutes later he returned. One of the men was dead, he said, and the other shot in the gut and in very bad shape. Mrs. Jones said, "Mr. Spencer is also dead. With his injuries I don't know how he lived as long as he did."

Matt ran over to Shade lying on the ground. Mr. Jones put a hand on his shoulder. "He's gone, boy, but you and Mr. Spencer made a hell of a good team."

Ranger Carter strode to the top of the ridge. He first treated, then handcuffed, the wounded shooter. He brought him down to Judge Layton. The judge asked whether Carter recognized the men.

"Two of the Miller boys from town."

"Any relation to former Deputy Miller?"

"First cousins," replied Carter.

Judge Layton hissed, "I should have expected as much."

A helicopter now passed by overhead and radioed down to the ranger. "The location is secure. I have two D.O.A.s and three injured," he reported.

"Copy that. The rescue team is five minutes out. We'll set down just north of your location and begin evacuation."

Matt looked down the mountainside with a long face. "There were so many things I wanted to tell Mr. Spencer. I wanted to thank him for believing in me."

"Matt, all the things you wanted to tell him, Shade already knew. Otherwise he would not have asked for your help," said Layton. "He knew how to read people. We can't bring him back to life, but we can honor his wishes for his daughter.

The rescue team arrived, and Matt ran over to his mother. He hugged her and let his tears flow.

"Mom, Mr. Spencer stopped the men on the ridge, but he's dead now." Lost for words, he hugged his mother some more.

Mr. Jones noted that this young man would go far in life.

Judge Layton agreed. "Oh yes, he will. And Mr. Spencer knew it from the very start."